A STUDY IN SCANDAL

Books by Caroline Linden

A Study in Scandal

CAROLINE

LINDEN

Copyright © 2016 P.F. Belsley

ISBN: 0-9971494-1-8
ISBN-13: 978-0-9971494-1-8

Printed in the USA

To younger sisters everywhere, but most
especially to *my* sisters

CHAPTER ONE

1822

Lady Samantha Lennox had been afraid of her father every day of her life.

Even as a child she had known to conceal this from everyone except her mother and siblings. To the world at large, the Earl of Stratford presented an image of austere urbanity, widely respected for his unparalleled collection of art and his ascetic personal habits. He was known as a proud man, true, but that was common among noblemen and was even accounted as his due.

Only his family knew his real nature: not merely proud, but utterly convinced of his own superiority. Acclaimed for his artistic eye, but ruthless in the pursuit of works he desired. Lord and master of a vast, wealthy estate, but cruelly unforgiving of anyone who didn't meet his standards. And when it came to his family, he expected nothing short of perfection.

His wife—whom he married for her beauty and her dowry, so that his children would be both handsome and wealthy—needed his permission for every purchase, and any item of her wardrobe that displeased him was promptly destroyed. His daughters were raised to be charming and pleasant at all times, never contradicting him or giving any bad impression of themselves, so that they might be a credit to him. His son was expected to be the epitome of a gentleman, well-educated, charming, always masterfully in control of every circumstance. The Earl of Stratford's wishes were paramount, and woe to anyone who flouted them.

And Samantha, his youngest daughter, was about to tell him she had stolen from him and lied to him to conceal that theft for seven years.

Even now, as she stood in her mother's private parlor listening to her brother and mother beg her to reconsider, she wondered how she'd got herself into this position. She certainly hadn't planned to become a criminal. But with one rash action, she had sentenced herself to a sort of purgatory, where the threat of discovery had weighed more heavily on her with every passing year.

Looking back, she could see how stupid she'd been. As a girl, she had fancied herself in love with Sebastian Vane, a good friend of her older brother Benedict, tall and handsome, loyal and kind. He lived across the river from Stratford Court, and the happiest memories of her childhood had been when Benedict would row them over to meet Sebastian in the woods, where they played at being pirates or explorers. When the earl was away, Samantha's mother permitted her children to do such things. But when she was ten, the earl discovered it and immediately forbade her from it, although Benedict was still allowed to go.

She was sure those youthful memories had fueled her infatuation with Sebastian, even after he went into the army and left Richmond. But it had been her sister Elizabeth's ill-fated romance that made her determined to marry as soon as possible, and Sebastian—being familiar, dear, and nearby—was her only potential suitor. Elizabeth, three years older than she, fell in love with a man named Robert Halley, who was kind, charming, and wealthy, but merely a gentleman. Lord Stratford refused his suit. Elizabeth wept and the countess pleaded, but the earl was implacable. "My daughter will not wed a commoner," he'd coldly said as he locked Elizabeth in her room to contemplate her error.

Samantha could not imagine the heartbreak her sister felt. She had vowed to wed as she pleased, and escape her father's control. But Sebastian was a commoner, and even worse, his father had gone mad and frittered away the Vane fortune until there was almost nothing left. Lord Stratford would never allow the match, and Samantha had impulsively embarked on a mad plan to force the issue.

Madness was the only way to explain it. She had taken leave of her senses and stolen four thousand guineas from a chest in her father's study. Late one night, she crept out of the house and smuggled the coins across the river to Montrose Hill House, Sebastian's home, where she gave them to his father. She reasoned that if Mr. Vane claimed it was a hidden reserve of funds, Sebastian would take the money. In her fevered dreams, he would then rush to ask her father for her hand in marriage, and if the earl refused, Samantha was ready to elope with Sebastian.

But nothing had gone right except the theft itself. Instead of blaming his recently sacked valet for the robbery, Lord Stratford publicly blamed Sebastian. Even worse, old Mr. Vane disappeared, along with the money, and soon people were whispering that his son must have killed him. Far from being his salvation, her stupid ploy had been his ruin. Horrified, Samantha had said nothing, and soon Sebastian was a pariah in Richmond.

And for seven years since, she'd said nothing—not one word of defense or protest against the vilification of a man she had loved since girlhood. The shame of it had grown a little more each year until it felt like a ball of lead inside her. But now Sebastian had fallen in love, with Miss Abigail Weston, and when Miss Weston came to beg for Samantha's help in clearing his name of those charges of theft and murder, it had been a great relief to finally tell the truth. She'd confessed all to Miss Weston and her sister, and to Benedict.

The last step to clear her conscience completely was to tell her father, and persuade him to retract his charges of thievery against Sebastian. Then Sebastian would be able to marry the girl he loved, and Samantha would feel that she had atoned for her sin against him. Even though she was determined, she knew the earl would be furious, and Benedict and her mother were doing their best to persuade her against it.

And to her shame, it was working. That lifelong fear of the earl lapped at her like cold dark water that could pull her in and drown her if she let it gain a hold on her. Benedict and Lady Stratford knew the whole story now, and they alone knew the earl's true nature. If anyone could discover a way to justify not confessing her sin, it would be they.

"It was the act of a child," her brother argued. "Surely we all deserve to let some of our childhood actions disappear without acknowledgment."

Samantha sighed. She *had* been a child to act as she had, but it was no excuse. "I was sixteen," she reminded Benedict. "Rash and unthinking, but old enough to know it was foolish and wrong," she added in honesty, as he started to argue again.

No one could deny that.

"It happened so long ago," fretted her mother.

Seven years ago next winter. "But it has not been forgotten," was her gentle reply. Not by others, and certainly not by Samantha herself. The knowledge that she had ruined a man, yet been unable to explain or apologize, had sat like a weight on her soul for seven long years.

"No, it has not." Benedict ran his hands through his hair, looking agonized. "But Samantha, think for a moment. You're stirring up trouble where none exists."

He meant trouble for her. No one had ever connected her to the missing money. Samantha was done thinking only of herself, though. "You're wrong, Ben. It caused Sebastian a great deal of trouble, and I cannot continue to keep silent, when what I have to say can exonerate him." Miss Weston's plea had upset the delicate balance Samantha had found between guilt and fear. "Because I said nothing, Sebastian endured years of lies and distrust. Even from you, Ben," she added as her brother closed his eyes.

"I thought…" His voice died and he hung his head. Benedict, who knew her so well, had suspected something seven years ago, though he never asked her about it. To protect her, he had turned his back on Sebastian, who had been his dearest friend since they were boys. It was another thorn of guilt, knowing that she had caused the rift between them. "I was wrong."

"We were both wrong." She laid her hand on his arm. "And we both owe it to Sebastian to make it right."

"How will this make it right?" he exclaimed. The countess made a horrified shushing sound, and Benedict glanced uneasily at the door. "Father hates Sebastian Vane," he said in a lower, though still impassioned, voice. "It's bad enough that you…" He hesitated, as if the word tasted unpleasant. "That you *stole* from him, but you did it to help Vane. Don't you see how that will enrage him?"

"It probably will." She had no doubt of it, and the thought of her punishment made her pluck anxiously at the trim on her sleeve.

"Then don't do this," said Benedict urgently. "Vane wouldn't want you to be hurt. I may not have been a good friend to him, but I know him well enough to vouch for that."

"I must." She shook her head, wishing they could understand. Even though she feared what the earl would do to her, she had to do this. Sebastian and Miss Weston were depending on her, whether they knew it or not. Perhaps that was what she had really been waiting for all these years: a chance to undo the damage she had caused and make it up to Sebastian. Now the moment had arrived and she would not shrink from it.

Her brother's shoulders slumped. "When?"

"Tomorrow morning. As soon as I can." The earl was away from Stratford Court for dinner tonight, and wouldn't return until late. Samantha would rather have got it over with immediately, but tomorrow would have to suffice.

Benedict pulled her into his arms. "Promise

me you won't go alone," he whispered against her hair. "For Mother's sake."

Over her brother's shoulder Samantha saw her mother. The countess was fighting back tears, her face pale and strained. "I promise," she said quietly.

He nodded and released her. With a murmured farewell to their mother, he left.

In the quiet, Lady Stratford came to take Samantha's hand. "I wish you wouldn't do this."

"I know." Together they walked to the settee and sat down, hands still clasped. "But I have to, Mama," Samantha said softly. "If I say nothing, it will cost Sebastian the girl he loves." The memory of Elizabeth's sobs as Stratford ordered Mr. Halley out of the house haunted her. "It will cost Miss Weston a lifetime of happiness."

"Perhaps not." The countess shook her head. "In a few years she may well thank you for saying nothing."

Samantha looked at her mother, whose marriage could hardly have brought her much happiness. "She's in love with him, Mama, and he with her. I—I think they will be happy together, if given a chance. And that means I could never forgive myself if I kept silent and prevented that chance." She leaned forward at the anguish in her mother's face. "I *can't* stay silent. It has been a terrible weight on my conscience, and now it would be unbearable, if I knowingly allowed it to ruin two people's happiness."

Her mother didn't argue further. Samantha told herself she was glad of that. After keeping the secret for seven years, she was both anxious and terrified to unburden herself. It felt like strength to contemplate facing the earl, but deep inside she felt she must be the weakest coward in the world to have avoided it so long. Even as she repeated, over and over, that it was the right thing to do, she worried that her nerve would fail her again.

The next day dawned clear and bright. Samantha took her time dressing, hoping a good appearance would please her father, and went downstairs.

Her brother was waiting, pacing the corridor some distance from the earl's study. He stopped when he saw her. "I suppose you're still set on this." She nodded once. Looking grim, he only sighed and picked up a dusty leather satchel from the floor.

Together they walked to the earl's study door. Benedict's expression smoothed into an inscrutable mask as he knocked. Samantha felt a burst of love for him. She knew most of the times Benedict had been admitted to the earl's study, it had been to get a whipping.

Lord Stratford was writing when they were admitted. His secretary backed silently out of the room, pulling the door closed behind him. For a few endless minutes, Samantha and Benedict stood at attention, waiting to be acknowledged. Her heart pounded. Father would be very angry. He had never whipped her, but she had never done anything this terrible. Perhaps her mother was right, and she should say nothing...

No. She gulped down her nerves. If he whipped her, she deserved it, not only for stealing and lying, but for letting an innocent man take the blame.

"What?" At last the earl spoke, in his usual abrupt and commanding manner.

"I have good news, sir," said Benedict before she could begin. Samantha darted a shocked glance at him. What could possibly be good about this news?

The earl didn't even look up. "For a change."

"Indeed," agreed Benedict. "To correct an old wrong."

Stratford's pen stopped. Slowly his gaze rose from his letter. "What old wrong?"

Samantha's stomach heaved, fearing her brother was about to confess to the crime himself. He'd done that many times when they were children, to spare her or Elizabeth from punishment. But Benedict kept his confident smile in place and avoided looking at her. He lifted the leather satchel. "I have recovered the funds from *The Death of Socrates*."

The name gave her a jolt of surprise; she'd almost forgotten it. But the stolen money had been payment for that painting, sold by the earl to another avid collector. How on earth had Benedict found it?

The earl's cold blue eyes narrowed on the satchel. His expression stole Samantha's breath; he looked like he could do murder in that moment. "How?"

"A fortunate guess." Benedict said it confidently, but even he couldn't withstand the piercing look from their father. He set the satchel gingerly on the edge of the desk. "Does it matter? Every guinea is here."

Stratford got to his feet and leaned forward, resting his hands on the desk, never once looking away from his son. "Yes. It matters. Those funds were stolen from this room several years ago, yet now you claim to hold them in your hands. Where was the money, and how did you recover it?"

Samantha wondered all those things, too, but this was her chance, perhaps her only chance, to make a clean breast of it. Before her brother could say another word, Samantha blurted out, "I took the money, Father."

The earl jerked, and complete astonishment flickered over his face. "You?"

Samantha nodded, ignoring the desperate glance Benedict threw her. "I did, Father." Her hands were shaking, so she hid them in the folds of her skirt.

Stratford was motionless. "May I ask why?" he asked in a deadly quiet voice.

"I gave it to Mr. Vane."

Fire flashed in her father's eyes. "I see."

She shook her head. "Not Sebastian Vane. Old Mr. Vane, his father."

For the second time he looked astonished. "The lunatic?"

"I was wrong," she said quietly. "I am very sorry."

Stratford looked at Benedict. "Did you know about this?" When Benedict hesitated, his father snapped, "The truth, boy."

She could feel her brother's despair, but to her relief he didn't try to take the blame. "No, sir."

"And you thought simply returning the money would make it all well again." The earl straightened to his full height and folded his arms. "I think less and less of your judgment every day." Benedict's jaw twitched, but he said nothing. "Go," said Stratford softly.

Benedict hesitated again. "Sir, Samantha was not wholly at fault—"

"I said go," repeated his father sharply. "You're afraid I might whip her? I would never raise my hand to a woman. I ought to have whipped you more, if this is the respect you have for me, but I fear it's too late for that. Go, and stay gone."

Benedict drew a breath as if he would argue, but Samantha made a small motion with one hand. This was her fault, and she deserved to bear the consequences. To her relief, her brother turned and left without another word, leaving her alone to face her father.

"I'm sorry, Father," she said, reciting the words she had rehearsed all night. "I was a foolish girl and acted as one. I am ashamed of myself for having maintained the lie so long." She wet her lips and steadied her voice. "I am telling you now because you must exonerate Sebastian Vane of stealing the money. No matter how much you dislike him, he is not a thief, and you have called him one for seven years—falsely, even if based on a reasonable suspicion."

She hoped the blow to his honor, and the return of the money, would be enough. If he refused to retract his charge against Sebastian, Samantha didn't know what she'd do. Standing on the street corner in Richmond and declaring herself the thief would only revive the horrid whispers about Sebastian, and enrage her father. She supposed she could call on Mr. Weston, Abigail's father, and assure him that Sebastian was no thief... if she was ever permitted to leave Stratford Court again.

"Why exactly did you take this money?" Her father's voice was more terrifying for being soft and even.

"I thought you wronged him," she said bravely. She still did, to be truthful. In the depths of his lunacy, old Mr. Vane had sold the earl a large piece of land—including the parcel which held the family crypt, where Sebastian's mother was buried—for a mere pittance. Stratford viewed a madman as beneath contempt, unfit to hold his lands, and he took full advantage of Mr. Vane, without caring one bit what it would do to Sebastian's inheritance.

"Ah, a woman philosopher!" He rocked on his heels and raised his brows. "What a pity I didn't consult you on that matter."

Her face burned at the mockery. "I was wrong to take the money, just as you were wrong to accuse him. I have made an honorable confession. I trust you will not wish the lie to endure a moment longer, Father."

His brows climbed even higher. "Is that what you require, my dear? But of course..." He smiled, cold and cynical. "My romantic daughter wants to clear Sebastian Vane, so he might have the girl who spurned your brother."

Samantha bit back an instinctive protest. It was true Benedict had once courted Abigail Weston, but she was quite sure her brother had never been in love with her. And Miss Weston was genuinely in love with Sebastian, which meant Samantha understood completely why she'd refused Benedict. In time, she was sure even Benedict would be grateful to her for that.

Stratford flipped his coattails out behind him and sat down, reaching for a fresh piece of paper. He wrote two lines and signed his name with a flourish. "Will that do? Is it sufficiently

18

humble, as I confess my great error in judgment?" He handed her the paper.

It was a stark admission of error, and even though it was exactly what she had wanted, it frightened her. "Yes, sir," she whispered. "Perfectly." This was not like her father, this overt courteousness. He had just sat down and done as she asked, without a word of reproach. He hadn't even raised his voice. A knot of dread twisted in her stomach. "Thank you, Father."

He bowed his head. "I am delighted it meets with your approval." She curtsied, thinking it was best to escape while she could, but it was too late. Her father got up from his chair again and came around his desk. He touched her chin, raising her face so he could study it. Samantha stood very still; her heart thundered. She had rarely been this close to him, and never with his unwavering attention fixed on her.

His eyes were as cold as a winter sky. "I see I failed with you," he murmured. "Perhaps even more than I failed with your brother. I don't quite know you, Samantha. It was always clear to me you were never as biddable as you ought to be, but you did appear to work at improving. Today, though…" He made a soft *tsk*, then continued in the same soft, leisurely tone that terrified her more than any furious shouting could have done. "It was all an act, wasn't it? All these years you were merely pretending to be the dutiful daughter. You chose that hotheaded arrogant Vane over your family. You stole from me—your own father—and lied about it for seven years. Even now I suspect you confessed only because you want to help Vane, or perhaps that parvenue heiress he hopes to marry. I can tolerate some soft-heartedness in a woman, but not soft-headedness." He released her and walked back to his desk. "And all this after I spoiled you so. I see now how wrong I was. You may go."

Her knees went weak with relief. That was all? She couldn't even react to the astonishing claim that he'd spoiled her, since no punishment had been threatened. "Thank you, sir."

As if in a daze she opened the door and let herself out. Blindly she walked through the corridors. She felt off balance and disconcerted, having braced herself for a tremendous blow that never came. Even the relief of having confessed was absent, leaving only a terrible confusion. Was that to be her father's only reaction?

"What happened?" Her brother's urgent question startled her so badly she almost screamed.

Mutely she held out the paper. Benedict seized it and then looked at her in amazement. "He wrote this?" She nodded. "What did he do to you?" She couldn't speak. "Samantha, what did he do to you?" repeated her brother, sounding panicked.

It broke her daze. "Nothing," she said.

He swore and grabbed her arm, pulling her behind him to their mother's suite. Lady Stratford was pacing when Benedict opened the door, but she stopped immediately at their entrance.

"She's told him," Benedict said, "but she won't say how she's to be punished."

Anxious hope leapt in Lady Stratford's eyes. "Perhaps he was content to have the money returned…"

Benedict shook his head, watching Samantha closely. "I doubt it."

"He said…" Her voice failed for a moment. "He called me a woman philosopher. He said he had failed with me. But he wrote that"—she motioned to the paper Benedict still held—"and said nothing of consequences." She looked from her brother to her mother. "That can't be all he intends to do, can it?"

"Perhaps," said the countess, her face as pale as milk.

"Doubtful," muttered Benedict.

Now Samantha began to be afraid. "What should I do?"

"Nothing," said her mother. "Do not show the slightest sign of fear or alarm. Act as if the matter is over and done with and no further thought of it will ever cross your mind."

That sounded difficult. It would only trade the burden of a guilty conscience for the tension of waiting, waiting, waiting for the axe to fall on her. She looked to her brother.

He didn't seem to know what to do. He ran his hands through his hair and avoided her gaze. "He told me to go, and stay gone. But I can't leave you here alone to face him—"

"What could you do?" She raised her hands at his expression. "What could any of us do?"

No one said anything. They all knew the answer: nothing. It had always been that way in the earl's house.

"Promise you'll send me word in London if he acts on this." Benedict's voice made her start. "I won't let him hurt you, Samantha. I swear I won't."

She shivered at the raw emotion in her brother's voice. If Benedict, who had endured innumerable thrashings as a boy at the earl's hands, feared for her safety, she ought to be terrified. But it was comforting to know he was on her side, even if she had no idea what he could do to protect her, or even what she needed protection from. "I promise."

CHAPTER TWO

For two terrible days silence reigned at Stratford Court. Samantha asked Benedict to send the earl's note to Sebastian before he left, but then there was nothing else for her to do. It felt as if she—and her mother—were both holding their breath, waiting to see what the earl would do.

Stratford, however, seemed unchanged. Not one word of the matter crossed his lips, and with some disbelief Samantha began to think he might have simply given up on her. It hadn't been his way, but if he no longer cared what happened to her, perhaps it wasn't worth his trouble and effort to punish her.

She should have known better.

At breakfast on the third day, Stratford finished his spartan meal and leaned back in his chair. "I shall be departing this morning."

"Indeed," said the countess with her usual cool composure. "I will notify the housekeeper about dinner. Will you be gone long, my dear?"

"A few days." His piercing gaze landed on Samantha, quietly eating her toast. "Aren't you curious to know where I'm going?"

The toast stuck in her throat. Samantha seized her tea and gulped it down, shooting a wide-eyed look at her mother. The countess's expression was blank. It was very unlike the earl to encourage inquisitiveness. "I didn't like to be presumptuous and ask, Father," she managed to croak.

His smile was flat. "No? A lesson learned, at last. This time I shall tell you, because it concerns you."

All the tension that had slowly ebbed during the last few days returned in full force, keeping her immobile in her chair as she waited for the blow. If Stratford had waited three days, he must have planned some awful new punishment for her.

"This week has been a most illuminating one," Stratford said. "And a humbling one. I realized I failed as your father, Samantha, failed miserably. And therefore, perhaps it's time I quit the field and found you a husband to guide your actions. A man with a firm hand, who won't tempt you to abuse his tender nature as you've done mine. I'm going to Penton Lodge to see the Marquess of Dorre. He's looking for a bride for his second son. I'm sure he'll take you without much protest."

For a moment the sunlight streaming through the windows seem to go out, leaving the room cold and gray. Samantha couldn't draw breath into her lungs. Lord Dorre's second son, Philip, was a handsome man, but with a brutal nature that even his father's immense wealth couldn't overshadow. Someone had once told her that he had put down a horse by shooting out each of its legs. There were whispers that he had got into a fight with another man and left the fellow crippled, unable to walk or speak. Every girl in Richmond would sooner claim a broken ankle—would sooner break her ankle in truth—than dance with Lord Philip. Samantha thought she'd rather be whipped than spend even one day with Philip, let alone marry him.

"My dear," exclaimed the countess in obvious distress. "Would you ally yourself with such a known libertine?"

That was true. Samantha had forgotten the tales of Lord Philip's debauched parties in London, attended by all manner of wicked persons. Lord Stratford must know of them as well, if she did, and for a moment hope reared its head. One thing Stratford could not abide was drunkenness and public indiscretion.

Slowly the earl turned to face his wife. She sat motionless, but her eyes were wide with appeal and her chin quivered. "Ah, I see," he said quietly. "You worry for her. 'Tis true, Lord Philip has a temper and a taste for danger." He looked at Samantha. "But our daughter is a clever girl, Lady Stratford. Clever enough to keep a secret from her entire family for seven years! I expect she'll learn soon enough how to please her husband and keep him from straying into immoral pleasures. I'm sure he'll be able to instruct her on his...tastes. Samantha is far past the age when she should be married anyway. It's my duty as a father to find her a husband, and I shan't neglect it any longer."

"He is cruel," whispered Lady Stratford. "Please, my dear—"

The earl slammed one hand down on the table, making the silverware—and his wife— jump. His eyes blazed with fury. "Remember your place, Lady Stratford!" He pushed back his chair and rose. "Tell your maid to fetch your trunks," he said coldly to Samantha. "You shall be married within the month." He turned on his heel and strode from the room.

A month. The words hung in the silence, as if a judge had pronounced a death sentence on her. A month.

Samantha stared at her plate in shock, her half-eaten toast forgotten. He meant it. God help her, he really might do it. So much for Benedict's hope that the return of the stolen money would soften his anger. He hadn't cared about the money at all.

Nor, apparently, about her.

"I will speak to him," came the countess's voice, so strained and quiet Samantha barely heard it. "I will persuade him against this. Perhaps not against marriage—" Her face contorted for a moment. "I should have suspected. You ought to have been married by now, mistress of your own home. If you had been, you would be safe—" She stopped and closed her eyes.

Samantha said nothing. She hadn't married yet because it hadn't pleased her father that she marry. And she had been in no hurry; when she married and left home, her mother would be left to face her father's tyranny alone. Aside from the fact that she had no suitors who satisfied the earl, Samantha had known, deep in her heart, that she was her mother's only remaining comfort.

If she married Lord Philip, her mother wouldn't even have the consolation of knowing she was safe, never mind happy. And she had a terrible feeling her mother would be unable to influence her father this time. There wasn't anything she could say, though, so she just nodded. There was a chance, after all—slim and wispy though it might be—that her mother would be able to sway her father into choosing someone kinder than Lord Philip.

All the courage that had propelled her to

confess and insist that her father retract his charges against Sebastian fled. She knew she'd done the right thing, but now...for herself... She was terrified.

"Mama." She met her mother's stricken gaze. "Perhaps Lord Philip isn't as bad as everyone whispers. Perhaps it's all exaggeration, or lies, or..." She wet her lips. "Surely a gentleman would not beat his wife," she said, more to persuade herself than because she believed it.

"No," said her mother at once. "I trust not. I cannot believe Stratford would sit by and allow his daughter to be beaten."

For all his faults, the Earl of Stratford had never struck his wife or daughters. Samantha tried not to think of all the times he had caned her brother. That was in the past now, as Benedict was taller and stronger than the earl and, most importantly, in London with his regiment of the King's Household Guard.

London. If only she could enlist in a regiment, or flee to distant relatives. But a daughter belonged to her father, even when she was of age. If her father signed a marriage contract he would see that she fulfilled it, and then she would belong to her husband. Even if Lord Philip wasn't as depraved as rumor held, Samantha had a feeling he would not be a kind or considerate husband.

"This is my fault," said her mother suddenly. "I should have seen how precarious your position here has become. Forgive me, darling—" She broke off and pressed her fist to her mouth.

"No, Mama. Any fault is not yours but mine." Samantha herself should have known. Benedict had bolted for London as soon as he was able. Elizabeth, three years Samantha's elder, had thrown herself into finding a husband as soon as she made her debut. Only Samantha had stayed behind, content with her sketchbooks and her secrets.

She summoned a deep breath and said a little prayer for courage. "May I call on my friend Lucy Walgrave?"

The countess blinked. "Today?"

"Why not? Perhaps she will know something about Lord Philip to put my mind at ease." Even as she said it, Samantha remembered that

Lucy was very fond of salacious stories. If Lucy had anything to relate, it probably wouldn't be good.

Never mind that, she told herself. It was more important to get out of the house and let her brain cool down so she could think what to do.

"Yes," declared the countess, a bit of color rising in her cheeks. "Of course you should go. It will be good for you."

Samantha waited until the earl left. In his absence, everyone at Stratford Court seemed to give a visible sigh of relief. The groom who brought the carriage around even gave her a slight smile as she climbed up, as if he knew she was clinging to sanity by a thin thread. For a moment Samantha wished intensely that her father would go far, far away, and never come back. Even the grooms pitied her, and they couldn't know her fate yet.

Lucy lived on the other side of Richmond, all the way across the river. Impulsively Samantha told the driver to set her down in town. She had long since stopped taking a maid when she went to Lucy's, and today she needed fresh air. "I shall walk from here. Fetch me from Miss Walgrave's house in one hour," she told the driver, who nodded and set the horses in motion. Samantha didn't know where he went, but today she enjoyed a fantasy wherein he went to a tavern and enjoyed himself over a pint of ale. As hard as it was to be the Earl of Stratford's child, it must be even harder to be his servant. She turned away and started down the street, trying not to think that this might be her last taste of freedom.

No. She mustn't think that. She walked along, oblivious to everything around her. If only Benedict were here. Stratford had ordered him to stay away, but there was no one whose advice she trusted more than Ben's...

It seemed like a sign from above, when she turned the corner and the first thing she saw was the coach bound for London. Samantha stopped in her tracks. Her breath grew short and her heart raced. No. The Earl of Stratford's daughter would never take a public coach...but perhaps that was why a mad urge to do just that billowed up inside her, choking her with longing. London was only ten miles away.

London, where her brother was.

Her feet started moving as her brain disposed of one argument after another. No one would know where she had gone…but her mother was the only one who would truly care, and Mama would understand. Her father would be furious…but he was away from home for the next few days. She could take the coach back to Richmond tomorrow and the earl would never know.

By the time she reached the driver, it seemed preordained that she would ask for a place on the coach; that he would have one left; and that the price would be almost exactly the sum in her reticule. When he added that the coach would depart in just a few minutes, Samantha only smiled. She climbed up and took her seat, keeping back from the window. Now that she had made her decision, she didn't want anyone to see her and try to stop her.

The coach was nearly full. The four other passengers gave her some curious glances, but no one spoke to her. They started off with a jerk, and she felt a small burst of excitement. This was an adventure, something she'd had very few of in her well-behaved, circumscribed life. She imagined Benedict's reaction when she appeared on his doorstep. He would be surprised, but also, she hoped, glad that she'd come to him.

The dust blowing through the windows made her cough; she would be filthy when she reached London. A discreet glance at her fellow passengers showed that she was the only one unprepared for travel. Everyone else wore sturdy boots and plain clothing. She felt a little out of place in her ruby spencer and pink dress, and unconsciously tucked her soft leather boots further beneath her skirts.

Before long the spires of London came into sight. Now she watched out the window in delight as the coach rumbled over city streets. They passed the expanse of Hyde Park, then the lush Green Park. The bustle of Piccadilly slowed the coach as they reached the heart of the city. Samantha's toes curled inside her shoes; she knew where Benedict's Guard regiment was quartered, but she'd never actually gone there, only to the parade ground nearby. Resolutely she forced aside the whisper of doubt. She could ask and be directed to the headquarters, and someone there would help her find Ben.

The coach finally turned into a yard seething with activity. It was hard not to gape in amazement as she climbed down. When her family came to London, the Stratford coach took them directly to the large house in Portland Place, bypassing this part of town. She didn't know exactly where she was now; the bustling yard and street beyond were far noisier, dirtier, and busier than Portland Place ever was.

But she had made it to London, and would not be deterred by something as trivial as being lost. Samantha went into the posting inn and asked for directions to Hyde Park Corner. She knew how to find the parade ground from there. The harried innkeeper pointed the way, and Samantha set out.

This London was a very different city from the one she had seen before. Omnibuses filled with people rumbled past. Elegant carriages with ladies out taking the air rolled past, on their way to the shops. Vendors stood on every street corner, calling out their wares. A ragged little girl with a basket of flowers ran after her, calling her "Your Worship" and begging her to buy a flower. Samantha was shocked by the child's spindly legs, bare below her too-short dress. She dug into her reticule for one of her last ha'pennies and handed it over in exchange for a bunch of daisies. The girl gave her a gap-toothed grin and scampered back into the crowd, crying to another woman to buy her flowers.

Samantha contemplated her daisies. They were slightly limp, as if they'd been picked some time ago, but still bright and cheerful. They made her smile.

"Your pardon, my lady!" A man sprang in front of her, sweeping off his hat and giving her a flourishing bow. "A moment of your time, please."

"Oh, I beg your pardon, sir…" She stepped backward, unnerved by his boldness. But he was handsome and well dressed, if a bit extravagantly, and perhaps people in London were more forward.

"It's about the girl." His eyes strayed after the flower seller, although she had long since vanished into the crowd. "With the flowers. Do you know her?"

"Not at all."

He sighed and shook his head sadly. "Have you ever seen her before today?"

"No."

He grimaced. "I was afraid of that! Drat and blast. I am Wilfred Humphries, private agent of inquiry." He tipped his hat again. "I've been charged with finding Lady Lucinda Radcliff, who was stolen from her parents as an infant and, one fears, sold on the streets of London."

Samantha gasped and twisted to look after the little girl, searching in vain for a glimpse of her ragged dress or flower basket. "Was that she?"

"Perhaps, perhaps." He urged her to walk alongside him. "I've been trying to catch her for some time now, but she's quick. And her parents—so worried, m'lady! As you can imagine, they're frantic to have her found. I hoped you might be a regular customer of hers and know where I could locate her."

"How do you know she's the girl you seek?"

He laughed pleasantly. "I don't! That's why I need to catch the child, to get a good look at her. Would you help me? She might be more willing to approach a lady such as yourself." Samantha hesitated, and he quickly added, "Think of her mother, the Countess of Ellsford, weeping brokenheartedly every night over her lost child."

"Lady Ellsford?" Samantha edged away, almost bumping into another man, much larger, who had come up silently on her other side. A chill of unease stole across her skin. "I think you must be mistaken. Lady Ellsford is past seventy. Her children are all older than I am." She was on the brink of suggesting he must be thinking of Lady Feinsworth, the matriarch of the only Radcliff family she knew, when the truth hit her. She raised her chin with a jerk and stopped walking. "I think you're lying."

Mr Humphries stepped close, and she realized he looked a bit like a rabbit, with a toothy grin and big dark eyes. Before she could recoil, he'd taken hold of her arm. "Perhaps it's a different Lady Ellsford. Come, dear, don't you want to catch the little street brat? Just in case."

"Let me go!" She tried to wrest free, but he had her. The hulking man on her other side crowded closer, trapping her with a thick arm around her waist.

"Come along, don't cause a fuss," cooed Humphries. "We won't hurt you…"

"You already are!" She struggled harder, but the big man squeezed her tighter. With a shock she felt his hand on her bottom. "Stop!"

"Not yet, just a bit further." Humphries smiled. His accomplice was holding her so tightly she could hardly breathe, and her toes were barely touching the ground now. "You're such a pretty girl, so lovely. Blond hair and green eyes, what a striking combination!"

"Nice tits, too," grunted the giant, who was still groping her bottom. "At least five guineas for this one, I wager."

"You'll be well treated, like a princess." Humphries pried her reticule out of her grip. "Just come with us quietly, or Billy will get rough. He's not used to dealing with ladies like yourself, his manners leave something to be desired—"

She managed to slap him, her hand shaking. "Help!" Samantha wheezed, terror stealing her voice. But the crowds that had surrounded them just a few minutes ago had thinned out, and the few people passing now kept their heads down.

Someone called out behind them and she craned her neck to see another man striding after them. "Help," she said again, a split second before wondering if he was part of the plot as well. The big man, Billy, cursed and yanked her up like a rag doll, quickening his pace while Humphries stopped and spoke to the newcomer.

Samantha's thoughts blazed through her brain like streaks of lightning, sharp and jarring and gone in an instant. She was an idiot. She was being kidnapped. No one was going to help her. No one even knew where she was. She had to do something to save herself.

She tried to call out again and the man carrying her shook her so hard her teeth knocked together. He was almost running now, hauling her along with his arm like a rope around her waist, and still no one seemed to pay them any mind. There was a shout behind them, and her captor glanced over his shoulder before taking a sharp turn and racing into a narrow, gloomy alley. Visions of being stuffed into a carriage and driven away, locked up and hidden until no one would ever be able to find her, filled her head. Her chest was being crushed by the meaty arm around her. She kicked, but her soft leather boots made no impact on his shins. Desperately she turned her head and sank her teeth into his shoulder. He wore only a grubby white shirt, and let out a vile curse as she bit him. His grip loosened and she managed to seize a lock of his hair and pulled with all her might.

"Bloody bitch," he snarled, dropping her.

Samantha fell hard, landing on her hip and forearm. Gasping from the pain, she scrambled backward, but he lumbered after her. "Ye cost me a guinea," he growled as he grabbed her by the hair and half dragged her down the sloping alley. He gave her a hard slap on the side of her head, and her ears rang. "Good riddance to ye."

And he pushed her, right into the river.

CHAPTER THREE

George Churchill-Gray was having a splendid day. Not only was the light perfect for painting today, he'd finally found the right mix of pigments for his latest canvas. Sadly, his next discovery had been that he was almost all out of two of them. It was an inconvenience, but a minor one; the day was clear and bright, so he put on his hat and headed for the print shop around the corner that sold the best paints. His fingers already itched to start work. This was going to be his best work yet, he could feel it in his bones.

He only noticed the girl because she wore a bright red spencer. She made a very lovely image, walking along the pavement with a posy of daisies in one hand, tilting her head from side to side as if she were lost, or perhaps new to

London and taking in the sights. Then he caught sight of her face, and realized it was the latter. She was marveling at everything around her, her eyes wide, her lips parted and curved in the most perfect air of enchantment. For a moment he admired the scene: the closely packed buildings cast into deep shadow, the bustling crowd flowing along the pavement like a human river, and then her, lovely and unhurried like a goddess stepped down to earth for the first time. It put him in mind of the work of Raphael or Titian, the way the light seemed to pick her out of the crowd and bathe her in a heavenly glow. He was almost distracted from his errand by the desire to watch her, to sketch her for a future work. Her face was Athena, he decided, youthful but serene, beautiful and noble.

As he stood admiring, the idyllic vision faltered. A man leaped in front of her, sweeping off his hat in a grand bow too elaborate to be innocent. The girl took a step backward, surprise evident in her figure. Unconsciously Gray's feet began moving in her direction.

But then all seemed well. The pair conversed

a moment. A stage lumbered through the busy street, briefly hiding them from his view, and when it had passed Gray saw that the girl was walking beside the man in the hat. Perhaps he knew her after all. She wasn't protesting or struggling. He hesitated, torn between the urge to get back to his studio and the lingering curiosity about the goddess in the scarlet spencer. He wanted another glimpse of her face. Not that she was any of his concern, a perfect stranger walking down the street. He'd learned his lesson the hard way, impulsively asking strange women if he could sketch them. At best she would look fearful and run the other way. At worst he'd find himself apologizing to a magistrate again. *Best be on to the print shop*, he told himself.

At the corner he glanced back, unable to resist entirely. The crowd had thinned a little, and he had a good view. Another man had joined the first, flanking the young woman. She no longer looked content, though; she kept edging away from them, and as Gray watched, the bigger man slid his arm around her waist. She jerked, trying to pull free, and Gray turned to follow without a second thought.

He lengthened his stride, not taking his eyes off her. She was struggling, but the men weren't letting her go, and they seemed to be almost carrying her between them. Gray cursed under his breath. What was the world coming to, when a woman could be picked up and carried off against her will in broad daylight, right in the middle of London?

As he got closer he sized up the men. The first was a handsome fellow, slim and short. He wouldn't be much trouble. The other man was bigger, uglier, and probably much stronger. He was the one holding the girl while the first man talked rapidly to her, petting her hand the whole while. Any doubts Gray had about her willingness vanished when she slapped him.

Gray broke into a run. "Pardon me," he called. "Are you in trouble, miss?"

She twisted to look back. Her eyes were green—and wide with fear. "Help," she said, her voice wheezing.

The bigger man pulled her off her feet and walked away, leaving the shorter fellow to face him. "Let go of the young lady," Gray commanded. His hands balled into fists.

The shorter fellow raised his hands calmingly. "She's a runaway," he said in a soothing voice. "A girl of good family, but with a wild nature. Her father hired us to find her and return her to him, safe and sound. Surely you don't want to interfere with the reunion of father and daughter? I certainly advise you against it, he's not a man to be trifled with…"

He took another look at the girl. The big man was hauling her down the street at a good clip, and she was still fighting him as best she could, kicking and pounding with her fists. But she was a slight figure, nothing at all to the hulking figure carrying her. "Oh? Her father asked that she be carted about like a sack of corn?"

"She's headstrong, good sir, liable to run away again without a firm hand."

It could be true. It could also be a lie, and if so, Gray would be abandoning a woman to unknown horrors. "Excellent," he said. "I'll just come along and see her safely returned to her family." He threw his arm around the shorter man's shoulders. "It will be my good deed for the day."

"That's not necessary," hissed the fellow, trying without success to wriggle free.

"It is to me," Gray assured him, holding tight. He caught sight of a constable on the other side of the street. "In fact, it looks like your man needs a little help with her. Let's gather a party to return her to the bosom of her loving father. I say, there's the very person we need. Constable!" He raised his free hand to hail the officer in question.

With a snarled curse, the man under his arm twisted, wrenching loose and sprinting after his partner. By now the thickset man had put quite a good distance between them, the girl still caught in his arm, still kicking her feet in protest. Gray took off after them both, shouting at the startled constable to help him prevent a murder.

The shorter fellow shouted something at his partner, who glanced back with an ugly glare. At the sight of the constable and Gray, he bolted down a side street. The first man kept going straight, but Gray veered after the second, keeping his gaze on the girl. When her captor realized he was still being followed, he ducked around another corner, in a narrow and dark alley. Gray slowed on instinct, as the constable was still some way behind him, but then he heard a curse, followed by a cry and a splash. He surged forward again and discovered that the alley led to a little inlet off the river. There was no sight of the big ugly fellow, but down the steep embankment in the swirling water of the Thames was the girl in the cherry red spencer, thrashing frantically but ineffectually against the pull of the water.

He stopped short. The water wasn't very deep here, but if she got pulled out much farther, he'd have to swim after her. He paused long enough to strip off his jacket, then slid down the slope and waded out to catch hold of her skirt. It was fine fabric, and tore in his hand as he tried to pull her back in. Gray swore under his breath and stepped farther out, until the water rose to his chest. She reached toward him, her fingers groping, and Gray recognized panic in her eyes.

He caught her arm and pulled, but his feet slipped on the mossy riverbank and he went under for a moment, almost losing his grip on her. The swirling water tried to suck her away again as he staggered back to his feet. The girl slid beneath the water's surface, her hands flailing frantically, and Gray dragged with all his strength, hauling her back until he managed to get his arms securely around her. For a moment he stood there with her against his chest, trying to catch his breath and steady his footing while she coughed river water all over his shoulder and clutched at his shirt.

"Ho there!" The constable had finally caught up, his round face red with exertion. "What's the fuss, sir?"

"Some villain pushed her into the water," Gray told him. "A big bruising fellow, about my height but a good four stone heavier. He must have gone that way. There was another fellow, short, well dressed, with a blue cloak. He disappeared into the Strand."

The constable hesitated. "Well, I expect there's no catching them now. Excellent work fishing her out. Do you know the young lady?"

Gray shook his head. She was shivering in his arms as he waded carefully toward the bank.

"Give me your hand." He reached out to the constable, who helped him ashore. A few curious passersby had already collected, peeping around the building into the narrow alley. He tried to put the girl back on her feet, but her knees gave out and she started to fall. Keeping an arm around her, he motioned to the hovering constable. "Hand me my coat." Again the officer did as he was told. Awkwardly Gray wrapped his jacket around the girl before lifting her again. Not only was she shaking, her dress had turned almost translucent. "We've got to get her warm and dry."

"Er…" The constable looked perplexed.

Gray shook his head to clear the water from his face. "My rooms are very near, just in the next street. I'll take her there and give her into my landlady's care. Will that serve?"

"I'll need her statement," protested the constable.

"Of course. You might also try to catch the men who tried to kill her."

The constable flushed at the hint of sarcasm, but he helped clear a path through the small throng of curious bystanders who had gathered.

Gray ducked his head near the girl's, hoping to shield her from their rabid stares. "Don't worry," he murmured. "You're safe now." She stared up at him, her skin bluish white and her wide green eyes unfocused and glassy. Even soaking wet and dazed, she was extraordinarily pretty. "Did you hear what I told the constable?" he continued, more to keep her attention than to impart information. "He'd best get after that man who pushed you into the river. Do you have any idea who he was?" No response, but she was definitely breathing better now. He hiked her a little higher in his arms, unconsciously appreciating the shape of her against him. Slim waist, round hips, lovely breasts. Her bedraggled bonnet hung by its ribbons, slapping wetly against his side with every step. Her hair was a mess but he thought it was probably light brown. She was pretty, well-fed, and expensively dressed.

What was a girl like her doing walking through the Strand alone?

Samantha began to emerge from her daze as

the strange man carried her through the streets. She had only vaguely registered his conversation with the constable. He'd saved her, at some danger to himself—he was just as wet as she was—and she remembered him shouting at the men who had grabbed her. Those men had meant her harm. This man, it seemed, did not, although she immediately reproved herself for thinking she knew anything. He might be merely a more clever version of the other men.

"Go ring that bell," he called to a boy sitting on a neighboring stoop. The lad jumped up and ran to obey. "Don't worry, you'll be warm and dry soon," he told her as he carried her up the few steps. "My landlady, Mrs. Willis, will tend you."

Samantha's teeth were chattering so hard she could only clench them together. Her mind and body both felt paralyzed by a combination of cold and fear. Part of her thought she should protest being carried along like this, by a man she didn't know, but the other—far larger—part of her found his arms rather comforting. And since she didn't think that her legs would support her if he did put her down, she made no protest.

The door opened and a pink-cheeked woman in a lace cap let out a cry. "Oh, good heavens, what have you done now?"

"I've been fishing," said the man holding Samantha. "See what I caught."

The landlady gawked at him, then flapped her hands. "Don't tease! Bring her in, bring her in! The poor dear—is she hurt?"

"We'll have to ask her." Carefully he carried her through the door held open by the woman, and into a small neat parlor decorated in shades of blue. He set her down on the small sofa.

The woman promptly pushed him aside to lean over Samantha, peering anxiously into each of her eyes. "She hasn't got that glassy look like Ned Davies had when he drowned. Can you hear me?" she said loudly, right by Samantha's ear. "Can you speak, dear?"

"Mrs. Willis, let the poor girl get her breath." Her rescuer accepted a length of towel from a young maid who ran into the room. He rubbed it over his head and let it fall around his neck, then sat down and pulled off his waterlogged boots. "Jenny, go fetch some hot tea, the river was cold." The maid nodded and rushed back out the door.

"Where did it happen? How did she end up in the river?" Mrs. Willis snatched a shawl from a nearby chair and threw it over Samantha. "And goodness—your boots!"

He looked down at his soaked footwear. "Some ruffian pushed her into the river and I had to get her out." He glanced up in time to catch her flinch. "He did push you in, didn't he?" he asked gently. "Did they hurt you?"

She could only stare at him. He had a kind face, on the long side, but with chiseled cheekbones and warm brown eyes. A drop of water ran from his dripping dark hair down his temple and he flicked it away with a swipe of his fingers.

He was quite handsome, she realized. Strong, too. Samantha remembered his big, capable hands pulling her from the water, then sweeping her into his arms, and shivered.

At her silence he gave Mrs. Willis a grave look. "We should summon a doctor."

That roused her at last. "No," Samantha whispered. She was perfectly fine, aside from being wet, cold, and still in shock over being almost kidnapped and then nearly drowned. She didn't know how to swim, and if he hadn't followed and saved her, she wasn't sure she would have made it out of the water. That alone disposed her to like him, and even trust him.

He raised his brows. "Are you certain?"

She nodded.

"Go on, dear," urged Mrs. Willis. "His Lordship only wants to help. He's a right decent gentleman."

Samantha licked her lips. "Lordship?" Heaven help her; did he know her family? She'd never live down the mortification of having to be dragged from the Thames.

The man in question looked like he wanted to roll his eyes. "George Churchill-Gray, at your service. No one calls me Lord George, and I beg you won't, either. I much prefer Gray."

"I'm a proper woman and I'll call you by your proper title," retorted his landlady. "Son of the Duke of Rowland," she whispered loudly to Samantha, as if Lord George Churchill-Gray weren't sitting three feet from her.

"Oh my." Samantha's voice faltered. The

Duke of Rowland. Her father hated Rowland.

"Pay it no mind," he said with an irked glance at Mrs. Willis. "What is your name? Your family must be worried about you."

Her brain froze. Her name. If she told him, he would take her back to her family. Suddenly Samantha felt like the biggest idiot alive; not only had she defied her father and gone to London without permission, she'd been robbed and almost killed. And her savior was Rowland's son, which would put her father in the duke's debt, to his mind. She could hear his furious upbraiding already, that she was incompetent, foolish, and a danger to herself. He'd have her wedded to Lord Philip within a fortnight, not a month. Mutely she shook her head.

Her rescuer rocked back in his seat. "What, you don't remember?"

She'd only meant to delay, but as soon as he asked that question, her mouth opened and she said, "No, I don't." And then, as if someone else had taken control of her body, she pressed one hand to her forehead and closed her eyes. "My head hurts."

There was a moment of silence. She peeked through her lashes and caught the nonplussed look on Lord George's face. It swiftly vanished when his gaze met hers. He gave her a smile, that confident, comforting smile she remembered seeing while he carried her. "I'm sure it will feel better soon. In the meantime, you are welcome to rest here. Mrs. Willis, will you bring something to eat? And some dry clothing." He got to his feet, running one hand over his head and sending some last drops of water onto his shoulders. "If you'll excuse me, I should change, and leave you to Mrs. Willis's care, Miss…" He hesitated. "I don't know what to call you."

Helplessly she stared at him.

"Well." He gave her a lopsided grin. "I hope it comes back to you, Perdita." He bowed awkwardly and left, leaving damp footprints on the carpet.

"Poor child," murmured Mrs. Willis. She gave Samantha a pitying glance. "I'll find some dry clothes for you—you're a dainty thing, but I might have some of my Mary's old clothes in a trunk in the attics. My eldest daughter," she added with a trace of pride. "Married a shipwright in Greenwich two years ago." She went to the door and leaned into the corridor. "Jenny! Where's that tea?" Without waiting for a reply she came back to the sofa and lowered herself to her knees. "Let's get you out of those wet clothes first, before you catch your death of cold. I hope His Lordship is clever enough to do the same, but one never knows with men…" She shook her head as she unlaced Samantha's walking boots. "He's a good boy, that one, but I vow he'd give away the shirt off his back and never once think of the cold. Another pair of boots, ruined! At least he had the sense to put the coat around you, dear, although I shudder to think how we'll get the stains out." She lifted the coat off Samantha's shoulders, whisking the shawl back into place a moment later. But Samantha caught the way her brows twitched upward at the sight of her clothing. Mrs. Willis recognized quality. Still, she said nothing about it, and Samantha found it easier to say nothing, too.

By the time the girl, Jenny, returned with a cup of tea, Mrs. Willis had helped her to a small bedroom at the back of the house. Together with Jenny, she peeled off Samantha's sodden dress, wrapped her in a nightgown that obviously belonged to Mrs. Willis herself, and put her into bed. "Drink, dear," urged the landlady as she collected the wet clothing and directed Jenny to take it to the kitchen for washing. "You'll feel better."

"Thank you." Her voice was hoarse. Samantha sipped the tea, knowing it was just a reprieve. Her wits seemed to be thawing along with the rest of her. She still had to find Benedict, but for now she only wanted to lie down. Her head did hurt, and she still felt cold. Surely it wouldn't be the worst thing in the world to delay a few hours. She could rest until her clothes were dry, then claim to have recovered her missing memory. She would thank the very helpful landlady for all her care, and ask her how to get to the Household Guard officers' barracks. Or even better, she could send her brother a note and ask him to come fetch her, so she couldn't possibly get lost again.

And if the very handsome Lord George Churchill-Gray protested and offered to see her safely into Benedict's care, she would politely decline.

Yes, she thought, finishing the tea and letting Mrs. Willis take the cup and tuck the blankets around her. That's what she would do... And on that thought, Samantha closed her eyes.

CHAPTER FOUR

By the time Gray got himself dried and freshly attired, Mrs. Willis had put the girl in bed.

"Fell asleep as soon as her head hit the pillow," she confided to him. "How frightening it must have been for her!"

"No doubt. Did she say anything else about the men who accosted her, or who she is?"

The landlady shook her head. "Not a word, poor dear."

Jenny, the maid of all work, appeared in the corridor. "Ma'am, there's a constable at the door, askin' for His Lordship."

"I'll be right there," Gray told her. "Don't let Perdita sleep too long," he said to Mrs. Willis. "If she got a terrible knock on the head, it's not good for her. Wake her up in a few minutes."

"Why, I never heard that! How is sleep bad?"

He shrugged uncomfortably; it was only his superstition, but he wouldn't be able to stop worrying about it until the girl was awake and talking again. "When I was a lad, a neighbor boy fell off a horse and hit his head. He complained of being terribly sleepy and went right to bed, but never woke. I don't want the same to happen to her. Humor me, please, Mrs. Willis?"

"Very well." She patted his arm. "So very gentlemanly to worry about her!"

He waved one hand and went downstairs to the parlor, where the constable was waiting. After the expected questions, none of which he could answer—*who is she? who were those men?* and *when can I speak to her?*—Gray leaned back on the settee. "Nothing's going to come of this, is it?"

The constable puffed up in indignation. "If we can find the men, and she'll swear against them in court, they'll be sent to Newgate." Gray gave him a cynical look, and the constable deflated. "Perhaps it might. She looks like a lady, don't she? It might have weight." He grimaced. "Of course, a lady might not want to swear in court."

"I'll be glad to swear in court. I saw everything."

The constable nodded and made a note. "Very good of you, sir. But I wouldn't expect much. The lady wasn't kidnapped, nor hurt badly."

Thanks to me, not to you, thought Gray. "Notify me if anything does turn up."

After he showed the constable out, he went to the landlady's room. The door was ajar, and Mrs. Willis was chattering away inside the room. Perdita must be awake. He rested his shoulder against the door and listened for a moment, wishing his landlady wasn't quite so voluble. He wanted to hear her voice again. She'd barely said a dozen words, and sounded more than a little confused while doing so, but her voice was soft and warm, while still bearing an unmistakably refined accent. It put him in mind of rosy sunsets over the lush green hills of Kirkwood, his family seat. She was a lady, he'd bet his last tube of vermillion on it. More than ever his fingers itched to sketch her. Perhaps, if she couldn't remember her name, she wouldn't decline his request in a burst of horror. He had saved her life, after all, surely that would offset any offense…

Mrs. Willis came into the corridor, interrupting his thoughts. "There you are, sir. The young lady's awake, as you asked, although she's got a touch of headache. I'm going to have Cook prepare a tisane for her—does a body good, Cook's tisane. But if you want to speak to her, go right in."

He waited until Mrs. Willis had bustled down the stairs, calling for Jenny. Then he tapped on the door, still ajar, and pushed it gently open. "May I come in?"

Perdita drew the blankets up to her chin. "Must you?"

Gray made a face. "No, but it's dashed uncomfortable to converse from out here. And shouting at you might make your headache worse."

"Oh." Her hair had dried in a mess of golden curls, falling over her shoulders like fractured sunlight. Late summer sunlight, bright and full of warmth. He tried not to look at it, but she was avoiding his gaze and blankets covered the rest of her. "I suppose, then…"

There was a high-backed armchair near the door. He pointed to it questioningly, and she nodded, a soft blush coloring her cheeks. Leaving the door conspicuously open, he sat down. "Thank you. The constable was here."

Instead of reassuring her, that seemed to make her more nervous. She worried her bottom lip between her teeth and blushed even pinker. "Has he caught them?"

"No, and I doubt he will unless you can think of anything that might help him discover them again."

"I thought not," she said on a sigh. "The first one—the polite one—told me he was searching for a lost little girl, like the one whose daisies I bought. Humphries, he called himself. He wanted me to help look for her in the crowd. But I knew he was lying when he said her mother was—"

He leaned forward when she abruptly stopped speaking. "Who?"

Now her face was ashen. "I don't know," she whispered. "Someone… I—I thought I

66

knew her... But I tried to walk away and then the other man was behind me and they wouldn't let me go."

Gray nodded. "And did they say what they wanted? Did they rob you?" She hadn't been holding one of those little bags women carried. Reticules—that was the word.

She stared at him a moment as if thinking. Her eyes were big and green, and with her hair down and the sheets clutched to her bosom, she looked like a young girl. He'd held her in his arms, though, and seen her soaking wet, and he remembered how very nicely grown she was. "Mr. Humphries took my reticule. They—they told me how pretty I was, and said I was worth five guineas."

Gray's hand curled into a fist. They had intended to sell her to a brothel. With her golden prettiness and air of gentility, she would have fetched a good price. But there was no reason to scare her. "Ah," he said lightly. "Gentlemanly villains."

The girl sank lower, her knuckles whitening around the blankets. "I don't think that. One of them touched me...*inappropriately* and spoke very crudely. The other man called him Billy, and warned me he wouldn't be gentle if I struggled…" She shook her head. "I was so *stupid,*" she said, her voice cracking on the last word.

"No." He leaned forward. "Do not blame yourself. A woman should be able to walk down a busy street in London without being accosted and molested."

"And nearly drowned." Her lips wobbled as if she were trying to smile. "Mustn't forget that part."

"Have you any idea why they did that?"

"I bit him, and yanked his hair." Pride warmed her tone. "He dropped me, but then I couldn't get away in time."

"Well done," he told her. "He deserved every bit of it."

"Yes." Her faltering smile died. "Do you think the constable will catch them?"

"He'll try." There was no reason to tell her more. "Your family will worry about you, and you must be longing to return home."

She licked her lips. Now that her color was coming back, Gray was vividly aware that she was very pretty indeed. Her mouth was the precise shade of a ripe peach. "I don't know…"

"Do you really have no memory?" he pressed, puzzled. He would swear she knew more than she was saying, but why would she pretend otherwise? Perhaps she really was a runaway. It didn't make him regret saving her from the ruffians who were hardly the sort any respectable gentleman would send after his daughter…or his wife…but then, perhaps that gentleman wasn't so respectable, or decent or kind. It was possible she had felt she had no choice but to run away. "Are you running from someone?" he asked on impulse.

She went alabaster pale again, and didn't speak.

"I won't send you back to anyone who might hurt you," he promised, though he had no idea what he would do with her. Even if he could persuade Mrs. Willis to let her stay for a while, it was a small house. Gray let the upper floors for his lodgings and painting studio, and there weren't any spare rooms. "But if you have friends or family who could care for you in more comfort, I want to help you back to them."

"I… I don't…" She bit her lip.

Again he thought of fresh peaches, juicy and sweet. Gads. For his own peace of mind he needed to deliver her to her family. "Do you live in London?"

Slowly she shook her head.

"Visiting, then. Were you going to meet someone?"

After a long pause she gave a slight nod. "I think so."

He grinned in relief. "Then I'm sure that person will be looking for you, when you don't turn up. Do you remember anything at all—where you were going, when you were to meet, a name…?"

For the longest moment she gazed at him with wide, unblinking eyes. She drew a breath, and Gray leaned forward without thinking, entranced by the color staining her cheeks and the clear green of her eyes. Who was she? In a blur of images, he imagined delivering her into the arms of a frantic family; snatching her from the grasp of a cruel guardian; saving her from an arranged marriage to a lecherous beast. He wanted to help this girl, and see her face glow with gratitude and admiration…to hear her invite him to call on her…to feel like her hero…

"My head hurts again," she whispered, seeming to shrink under the covers.

Gray sat back, feeling like he'd been dropped from a tall height. She wasn't spinning fantasies of him as a dashing and brave hero, but suffering from a terrible experience and possible injury. "I'm sorry," he said at once, giving himself a mental slap. "You should rest some more. But not too long," he added, thinking again of Dickie Russell, who went to sleep and never woke.

"Thank you." She slid lower on the pillows in blatant suggestion that he leave. The blankets were clutched up tight under her chin.

Gray rubbed his palms on his knees, then rose and left, pulling the door closed behind him. Mrs. Willis met him in the corridor. "How is the young lady?"

"She said her head hurt. I think we should send for a physician, regardless of what she protests."

The landlady's forehead creased. "Of course! Naturally we should, I'll send the boy directly. But who is she?"

Gray hesitated. "She doesn't remember."

Mrs. Willis's eyes popped wide. "What, not a bit?"

"Shh!" Gray put up both hands to shush her, picturing the poor girl listening to them from under the blankets. "She says not."

"Well, I never! When she wouldn't say earlier I thought it was all a dodge."

He didn't volunteer that he thought much the same thing. "Either she truly doesn't know—she did suffer a vicious assault—or she doesn't want to tell for some reason." He lowered his voice even more. "Frankly I suspect it's the latter. She looks frightened."

His landlady gasped. "Of what? Do you think those ruffians may come back looking for her? Oh, what will become of us if they break in the door!"

"I don't think that will happen," he said, to no effect. Mrs. Willis was worried now, and had an imagination able to supply an endless series of horrid visions.

"I don't want that sort of trouble in my house! I'm a widowed lady, m'lord, with Jenny to look after. Her mother is my own sister, you know, how could I ever face her again if I allowed her daughter to be carried off to suffer unspeakable horrors?"

"Mrs. Willis," said Gray firmly, "that won't happen. Calm yourself."

She gave him an affronted look. "Then what are we to do? I don't like to turn out the young lady, but—"

"We can't turn her out."

Her eyebrows went up at his brusque tone, and she began a brief but furious argument in whispers about the lack of beds, the possible danger, Christian charity, the propriety of her house, and—of all things—the cost of tea. Gray, having recognized the exercise as a negotiating tactic, ended it by promising to pay for not only the doctor but any other expenses and inconveniences caused by Perdita's presence, including a bit extra for the work Jenny would be put to changing linens and such, at which point Mrs. Willis nodded in acceptance. Gray started to go upstairs, feeling like getting into bed and pulling the covers over his head as Perdita had done.

"But that doesn't answer where I'm to put her," his landlady called after him. "I haven't got a bed to spare, my lord!"

Gray ran his hands through his hair and barely refrained from cursing. "Put her in my bed." She let out a horrified gasp. "Not *with* me," he added testily. This was why he kept to his own rooms when in the house. "I'll sleep in my studio." There was a battered chaise longue up there, although the floor might be more comfortable. At least his feet wouldn't hang over the end of the floor. "Have Jenny make up a cot and sleep near her. She can help if Perdita falls ill in the night and ensure everyone's reputation is kept pristine."

"Well." She raised her chin, somewhat mollified. "I suppose that will do."

Gray exhaled in relief. "Thank you, Mrs. Willis. I'll remove my things so you can shepherd her upstairs."

"This is just for tonight, Lord George?"

"Absolutely," he said, slinking toward the stairs. He had no idea what he would do with

Perdita tomorrow. He just knew he couldn't push her out the door as she was now, all pink cheeks and flustered blond curls and wary green eyes. Most likely a night in strange surroundings would persuade her it was better to go home, and her memory would enjoy a full recovery by morning.

She sighed. "Very well. But supper will be late if Jenny has to watch over her."

The prospect of eating with Perdita caught his attention, but the certainty of dining with Mrs. Willis promptly dismissed the idea. "I'm dining out tonight," he told her, then bounded up the stairs. It took only a few minutes to transfer the necessary supplies up to his studio on the top floor, then he seized his coat and left the house. A soft murmur of voices from the rear of the first floor made him pause again before he resolutely strode onward.

Perdita would go home tomorrow. And he would do well to keep his distance from her until then.

CHAPTER FIVE

By the time sun poured through the windows the next morning, Samantha had gathered her courage.

She must go home. Not only was she taking terrible advantage of the kindness of Mrs. Willis and Lord George Churchill-Gray, she saw now that the whole enterprise was a fool's errand from the start. Her best hope at this point was to return as soon as possible and throw herself on her father's mercy. The mere idea filled her with terror, but perhaps a flood of tears would achieve what dignified pleas and careful queries could not.

First she had to apologize to her hosts, in particular Lord George. It had taken her a little while to realize that when Mrs. Willis urged her upstairs to a larger bedroom, the landlady was escorting her to His Lordship's apartment. There was nothing overtly male about it, being two good-sized but plain rooms furnished simply though comfortably, but as soon as Samantha sat on the edge of the large bed, she knew. It smelled faintly of sandalwood and shaving soap, like her brother used. And when she asked, Mrs. Willis confirmed that the gentleman had given up his rooms for her.

"He'll bide upstairs in his studio," Mrs. Willis said, plumping up the pillows. "He insisted, m'lady, and Jenny will be here if you need anything. You're not to be troubled. Rest your dear head so you might remember everything."

Samantha had been sure she wouldn't sleep a wink in a strange man's bed, but she did—except for the two times during the night when Jenny inexplicably poked her awake, sleepily inquiring how she felt. But now it was morning, her dress had been returned to her, washed and mended, and she had no earthly excuse to delay.

She climbed the stairs, nervously rubbing her palms on her skirt. Despite the cleaning, it still bore faint stains from the dip in the river yesterday, driving home how shabbily she had repaid Lord George's heroics. Composing her expression, she raised her hand and knocked on the door.

It opened an inch and a single eye met hers. "Are you alone?" he whispered.

Samantha drew back in trepidation. "Yes…"

"Thank God." He swept the door open and bowed. "Come in."

"Oh no, I…" Her hands were damp against her skirt again. "I wanted to thank you, and to apologize…"

"I would be happy to accept both thanks and apology, but above all else, I wish to avoid Mrs. Willis," he said in the same half-whisper. "Will you come in? You may leave the door open."

She stared. He was mad. He was also barely dressed, wearing only trousers and a shirt, which billowed loosely over his chest and hung open at the neck. The sleeves were rolled up, exposing his forearms, and he wore scuffed boots on his feet. His long brown hair hung almost to his shoulders, and stubble shadowed his jaw. "Why do you want to avoid Mrs.

Willis?"

He glanced past her as a bit of conversation floated up the stairs; the landlady was scolding Jenny about the laundry. "She's the worst of my least-favored tutor and my childhood nurse, melded into one person. Will you come in?"

The proper answer would be *no*. Slowly, Samantha stepped over the threshold.

Lord George closed the door halfway, then strode back across the room. "Did you sleep well?" He caught up a smock and flung it over his head.

"Yes, thanks to you." Covertly she watched him tug the smock into place; it hung past his hips and was stained with paint, mostly on the right side. It didn't hide his forearms, or his long-fingered hands, and the act of pulling it over his head had ruffled his hair into a tousled mess, as if he'd just got out of bed. It was indecent to watch something as intimate as this, and yet she couldn't stop herself. "I understand you gave up your rooms for me. Thank you."

He waved one hand. "I could do no less." His eyes connected with hers for a second before veering away. "It's frightfully rude of me, but do you mind if I work while we talk? I was in the middle of a hurricane."

"Not at all," said Samantha automatically.

He grinned, a palette of paint already in his hand. "My profuse thanks for tolerating the eccentricity of a painter." He leaned forward and daubed his brush on a large canvas set up facing the windows.

Uncertainly Samantha looked around the room. She had expected a tiny garret, up here where one normally found servants' quarters, but it was not. The ceiling was lower than downstairs, but otherwise it was spacious, with three windows right in a row, as if three small rooms had been knocked into one. The result was a sunny space, cluttered only with pots of paint, paintings of various sizes, blank canvases, two large easels, a mismatched pair of wooden chairs, and—shoved back in a corner and still bearing signs of having been slept on—a green chaise longue. From under her lashes she took another look at her host. There was no way a man of his height could have slept comfortably on such a piece of furniture.

But he gave no sign of resentment. All his

attention was focused on the canvas. "What are you painting?" she ventured after a few minutes of silence.

"A shipwreck," he muttered, tossing aside his brush and reaching for a small knife. He scraped some paint off the canvas, wiped the knife on his smock, and went back to the brush.

"May I look at it?"

He looked up, his forehead creased in surprise. Instantly Samantha took a step in retreat. "I'm sorry. It was impolite to ask—"

"No, come see." He beckoned. "It will look better when it's done."

The centerpiece of the painting was a sailing ship, broken on the rocks. A wild storm whipped up the sea around it, the waves surging in angry white spills of foam over the decks and forecastle, and angry dark clouds boiled across the top half of the canvas, slashing rain down. The sails drooped from the snapped masts like a flag of surrender. In the foreground, right at the bottom of the canvas, was a young woman dragging herself from the sea onto a narrow beach. Her dark hair blew across her face as she turned to face the wreck. Her scarlet dress was a spot of vivid color in the otherwise dark and angry scene.

If Samantha had anything to thank her father for, it was an appreciation of art. Stratford Court was filled with masterpieces both old and new, and when the earl was in a charitable mood, he would wax eloquent about technique and composition. For a while, Samantha had had the idea that if she showed some artistic talent, her father would be fonder of her, and treat her with more affection. It hadn't happened; her abilities were sadly limited to doodling and sketching. But she could recognize talent, and Lord George had it in spades. She could envision this work—or more likely a large-scale version of it—hanging in one of the drawing rooms at Stratford Court, opposite the serene river view. Her father enjoyed such juxtapositions.

She could hardly tell him all that, though. "How dramatic," she said after a moment. Her eyes lingered on the girl who had escaped calamity.

Lord George's face grew grim. He took up

the knife and scraped more paint from the clouds.

"It's quite good," Samantha added hastily, sensing that her comment had been taken wrong. "Splendid, really. The waves are so well rendered, and the light in the clouds is exquisite."

"Do you think so?" He slanted a sideways glance at her.

She nodded.

His expression eased. "If it all comes out as planned, I'll submit it to the Royal Academy for next summer's exhibition. I put in four this year, and have hopes this one will turn out better than any of those."

"Oh, I'm sure they'd accept it," she said eagerly, but without thinking.

"Why do you say that?" He tilted his head at her sudden appalled silence. "You sound familiar with the Academy."

She was. Her father spoke of it often, generally to heap scorn on the committee who selected works. But now that the moment of confession was here, Samantha knew she didn't want to tell Lord George, with his rumpled hair and kind eyes and strong bare arms, who she was. She could thank him and take her leave, and he would never connect her with the stern and cold Earl of Stratford.

Nor was she ever likely to cross paths with a painter once she was married to Lord Philip.

"I meant it's so strong, artistically, with such vigor and passion, how could they not take it?" she parried, trying to smile normally.

"Ah." He didn't look fooled, but he also didn't press her. "I certainly hope they do. It would please my mother to no end, and reassure my father that I'm not wasting his funds."

His father the Duke of Rowland. Samantha retreated across the room, knowing she should get on with her apology and leave-taking. "Your father supports your painting?"

"With some mystification," he said, working at the canvas again. "He'd understand better if I joined my brother Rob in the Home Office, or took after my brother Tom and went into the army. I suppose he'd even endorse it if I wanted to breed horses, like Will."

"Three brothers?" Samantha said faintly.

Good heavens, no wonder Stratford hated Rowland. Four sons!

Gray laughed. "Four infernal sources of worry, aggravation, and despair! And a constant drain on his purse." He shook his head, but his easy smile remained. He spoke in humor.

She wet her lips. "Better than four daughters."

He paused, his dark eyes flickering her way for a moment. "I wouldn't know. No sisters. My father used to say he wanted a daughter or two, that girls wouldn't break their arms riding strong-willed horses or put dead rats in the tutors' boots or get into his brandy and decide it would be brilliant fun to try on the suits of armor in the gallery and attempt a joust." Samantha smiled at that one, and Gray's grin returned. "No, he said he'd much prefer to have a dainty little girl who served him tea and let him spoil her with new bonnets and hair ribbons."

Perhaps a man with four sons would deign to spare some indulgence on a daughter. She turned away, studying some of the other sketches and paintings that filled the studio.

"But you're an artist. I suppose none of those other things appealed."

"Not a one," he said promptly. "And not merely for being already done by my brothers. Besides, I'd be rubbish at all of that. Just as they'd be rubbish at this." He paused, lowering his brush. "Although some days it seems I'm rubbish at this, too."

"Oh, you're not!" Samantha protested. "These are wonderful!" She revolved on the ball of one foot, sweeping her hand around the room.

"Bah." He stabbed his brush into a nearby pot and tossed down the palette. "I had it on my fingertips and then it was gone."

"Oh yes, I do hate that." She nodded in sympathy. "But it will come back."

He looked up. "You paint."

Startled, she shook her head.

"Draw?" He grinned. "Come, I can tell you do something. Watercolor?"

"Not well." She cleared her throat. "A little drawing…"

His eyes lit up. "Brilliant!" He snagged a sketchbook off a nearby table and held it out.

"You've seen my work, Perdita," he pointed out.

The name stung her. Perdita, lost one. All the same, she didn't want to be found, not yet. A bit defiantly, she took the sketchbook and charcoal pencil he handed her, and sat down on one of the chairs. "I'm not very good," she declared, bending over the paper. "You'll be sorry you wanted to see. It's nothing to what you do."

She drew in silence, acutely aware of him watching her. Thanks to her father, she'd never had a suitor—not that Lord George was watching her that way, or ever would. But just being this near him, with his attention fixed on her, made her nerves hum and her cheeks flush the way she imagined a suitor's regard would do. "There," she said in a husky voice.

He leaned over and looked. Samantha tilted the sketchbook to show him what she'd drawn, a whimsical little rabbit sitting back on her haunches, head tipped quizzically to one side, one ear up and one ear down.

"Very good," said Lord George warmly. "What's he unsure of?"

"She." Samantha regarded her doodled rabbit. "You."

He shot her a glance, a laughing look from beneath his absurdly thick eyelashes. "Me? Surely not." He reached for another pencil. "I know what's got her at a stand…"

Samantha let him take the sketchbook. He sat on the chaise and propped one boot on the opposite chair, settling the book atop his knee. She watched his hand as he drew, his fingers barely holding the stubby pencil as he worked. His hands themselves were marvels, to her surreptitious scrutiny, as finely sculpted as anything any artist ever carved from marble, but warm and golden with life. Short hairs scattered over the back caught the light as he shifted the pencil, now shading, now drawing something curved, then straight. They were strong hands, capable and gifted and confident.

"That's better." He turned the book around and displayed it.

Flustered that she'd been staring at his hands and wondering what his skin felt like, Samantha stared at the sketchbook blankly for a moment. Then she burst into laughter. "How ridiculous!"

Now another creature sidled up to her rabbit, a lean and sinuous skunk, instantly recognizable from the deft shading. His pointed head angled toward the rabbit, his tail unfurled behind him suggestively, and a smile that could only be called seductive adorned his face. With one hand he held out a single daisy toward her shy and perplexed rabbit. And where her drawing had been done in a few careful lines, the skunk leapt off the page in full glory, from the gleam in his eye to the wrinkles in the petals of the tiny daisy. If she'd ever wondered how much talent she truly had, this put a firm end to it. Next to a real artist's work, hers was the drawing of a child.

At her laugh, that artist grinned. "Come now, he's a handsome fellow!" He ran the pencil across the paper, and grass sprang up in its wake. A few more lines and a tree sprouted behind the skunk. "Surely she's tempted…"

She took back the book and pencil. Behind her rabbit she drew another, a little taller, with its ears angled sharply forward and his expression angry, like a disapproving papa glaring at the rakish skunk. Without a word she turned it around.

"Ah," he said wryly. "I see. But perhaps…" He took the sketchbook and rubbed something with his thumb, then drew again. "He's not as bad as he seems."

This time Samantha's smile was bittersweet. Somehow he'd altered the skunk's expression, making it less sly, and now the skunk's free hand lay over his heart. No longer a rake but a hopeful swain. "He's still a skunk."

Lord George added a few more flowers to the posy in his skunk's hand. "A rabbit and a skunk aren't so dissimilar, once you overlook the fur."

"Not everyone can overlook the fur." She took back the book and ripped out the page. "I think you made more of it than I intended."

"What did you intend?"

"Nothing," she said after a moment. "Drawing little animals is just a habit of mine…" There was little else to do at Stratford Court. No one came to call and there were few neighbors she was permitted to visit.

Lord George was quiet for a moment. "What other habits do you have?"

"The only one worth admitting is playing on the pianoforte. I'm usually very dull and quiet," she said softly.

"That sounds a tranquil life."

The mild interest in his tone made her jerk up her head and meet his eyes. He was watching her far too closely, and abruptly Samantha realized what she'd told him. She lowered her gaze.

He leaned forward. "You remember more than you let on, don't you?"

Her face burned. She was the worst sort of person, willing to lie to him and trespass on his kindness and hospitality, all so she could delay facing the consequences of her reckless actions. And still this was one of the most enjoyable mornings of recent memory. Admitting her deception would mean it was the only such morning—but no, that was wrong. It was yet one more thing she had stolen, and therefore had no right to enjoy. Almost against her will, her chin dipped down: *yes*.

"Perdita, look at me." When she stubbornly kept her eyes averted, he reached out and touched her chin. His fingers were gentle as he turned her face toward him again. "Are you running away from someone?"

She thought of her father, and then of Lord Philip. "It's difficult to explain."

"Are you afraid?" he asked, his voice still soft. "I won't make you go back."

It was a hollow promise. Samantha knew she couldn't stay. He might not make her go back, but she had no other option. Everyone she knew was too awed by her father to take her in and shelter her, and she had nothing of her own to support herself. Even her idea of finding Benedict was foolish. What could her brother do, that she could not do herself? Her cherished hope that he would somehow help her avoid marriage to Lord Philip began to look silly and naïve.

Sooner or later she must return to Stratford Court. As much as she wanted it to be later, every hour she delayed made the eventual reckoning that much more terrible.

"Thank you," she told him, ignoring his questions and latching on to his last words. "You're too kind."

Lord George's mouth curled up on one side.

"Will you at least tell me your name? I can't believe it's really Perdita."

She blushed again. Obviously she could not tell him the full truth, or he would know who she was. But perhaps… "Samantha," she murmured.

His face lit up with boyish delight. "Samantha." With a flick of his wrist he caught her hand and pressed it lightly, bending forward to brush his lips across her knuckles. "A pleasure to make your acquaintance, my lady."

Fierce and swift, longing rose up in her chest. Oh how she wished…but that was more foolishness. She rose to her feet, suddenly anxious to leave. "I do apologize for imposing on you. I can never repay your kindness in pulling me from the river, to say nothing of the fact that you took me in and gave up your own quarters for me."

He stood, too. "You owe me nothing." He paused, lowering his head to see her better. "If you are ready to go home, I will take you."

She didn't want that, but it was the best she could hope for. Valiantly she nodded. "If you could help me find the coach, I would be grateful. I'm not precisely sure where it leaves from."

"Of course. What destination?"

Samantha gulped. She would probably never see him again, this charming artist with the too-long hair and the laughing eyes. And she would do well to remember that it was best that way.

"Richmond."

CHAPTER SIX

Gray washed off the paint and dressed in proper clothes, his spirits mixed. On one hand, he was relieved that she hadn't suffered a debilitating knock on the head and knew both her name and where she was from. It had occurred to him that it might not look good if she really was a runaway or lost person, and he did nothing to return her.

But on the other hand, anyone could see she wasn't eager about it. He hadn't missed the spark of longing in her eyes when he rashly promised that he wouldn't make her go back to something dreadful. She hadn't taken that as an invitation to confide in him, though, so he saw no choice but to put her on the coach to Richmond.

At least he knew her name now. Samantha

suited her much better than Perdita.

She was waiting in the parlor when he finished tidying himself. He paused in the doorway, struck by how still and quietly she sat, ankles primly crossed, hands folded in her lap. Her head was turned, her gaze directed out the window, and his gaze fell on the pale slope of her neck, exposed under the thick twist of blond curls, now smoothed into simplicity. Her bonnet must have suffered irreparable harm, for she held a plain straw bonnet he recognized as one Jenny wore. No doubt Mrs. Willis would want a guinea to replace it.

"Are you ready?"

She started at the sound of his voice, but got to her feet. "Yes." She tied on the bonnet, hiding her face.

"It's not far," he told her as they set out.

"No?" She smiled wistfully. "It's a lovely day, I wouldn't have minded a long walk."

Gray nodded, indicating they should turn at the next corner. It would add some minutes to the trip, but he had an irresistible urge to talk to her. "I've no idea when the coaches leave; you may have to endure a wait."

"I don't mind that, either."

His conscience made only a token objection as he steered her on yet a longer detour. Normally it would take no more than a few minutes to reach the Spotted Dog in the Strand, where the coach stopped; instead Gray turned up Drury Lane, toward Covent Garden. "I'm delighted you weren't badly injured yesterday. Someone at home must be worried about you."

She didn't answer for a moment. "My mother will be."

He nodded. "Mothers always are. Once my brother Will and I went off on a jaunt. We must have been all of eight and nine, and decided to go in search of buried treasure, having heard a rumor about ancient Vikings landing on a nearby beach. So we saddled our ponies and took some shovels, and away we went. Unfortunately the shore turned out to be much farther away than we expected, and then it began to rain, and Will had forgot his compass…" He shook his head when she gave him a horrified glance. "We were two sad and sorry lads when we straggled back home. Mother was beside herself, and Father was in a fury."

Her face grew pale. "Were you punished badly?"

"No." Gray grinned in vindictive memory. "Rob and Tom were, though. They wanted to get rid of us, two annoying younger brothers, so they talked loudly of Viking treasure where we could overhear."

"But you…?"

"Put to bed with warm milk while Mother read to us. She was frightened we would fall sick." He paused. "She did make us stay in the next day too, which wasn't as satisfying."

After a moment she smiled. "Fortunate lads."

They had reached the market, teeming with vendors and people strolling, shopping, admiring wares, haggling over baskets of fruit. He edged closer and offered his arm. "It's busy today," he coaxed, hoping it wasn't too transparent.

Samantha's eyes had rounded in amazement, which turned into delight. "What variety!" Absently she tucked her hand around his elbow, letting him lead her through the throng as her head swiveled from side to side, taking it in. "I've never seen the like."

Gray filed that information away with the rest. To the best of his recollection, a coach left every three hours or so, which Gray felt absolved him of any duty to take her directly to the inn, where she'd surely just sit and wait. She intrigued him and she puzzled him and he wasn't able to resist the urge to spend just a little more time with her. He couldn't forget the way her face lit up at his sketch of the skunk. He took the longest possible route through the market, savoring her wide-eyed marvel at the Punch and Judy show. He bought an orange and peeled it for her, laughing at how she tried to eat it without getting juice all over her gloves before finally stripping off one.

"It's ruined anyway," she said with a small surprised laugh. Gray got the impression such an act was out of character for her even though she took obvious pleasure in it.

But every time he tried to lead the conversation to her home and why she was alone in London, she went quiet. He began to feel a little worried about that. She didn't look afraid—if anything she looked extremely composed. He shook off the doubt; perhaps it was regret for the whole misadventure, and she found his questions, however subtle, rude and embarrassing. He'd promised he wouldn't make her go back if she didn't want to, and yet she had only asked him to help her find the coaching stop. Finally, reluctantly, he turned them in the direction of the Spotted Dog.

Samantha felt a twinge of regret when she recognized the coaching inn in front of them. She suspected Lord George had taken a roundabout way here, to her private—though somewhat ashamed—delight. Who could blame her, though? He was even handsomer in full daylight, decently dressed and with his long hair slicked back beneath his hat, and his attention was fixed on her in a way that sent her imagination running amok. It was easy to pretend he was a suitor, making her laugh and buying her oranges and touching her hand at every opportunity. He was everything she'd ever dreamed of a suitor being, and for a few minutes she refused to remember that she was practically engaged to marry Lord Philip, who was nothing she'd ever dreamed of in a suitor, let alone a husband.

Yet the end of the idyll also filled her with relief, because every moment she clung to Lord George's strong arm tempted her to tell him everything. He'd said he wouldn't make her go back, which might mean he would help her find her brother, find a place to stay, find a way to change her father's mind and change her life.

A glance at his face swept that nonsense from her mind. How could she ask this decent, honorable gentleman to put himself at risk to help her? Thwarting her father would be a very dangerous proposition, and Samantha already liked Lord George far too well to do that to him. Even asking him to help her find Benedict would be wrong. It was far better that she remain a mystery to him, as much as possible. "Thank you for all your kindness," she said as they approached the inn.

"It was my honor." He paused. "Are you quite, quite certain you wish to go back? I can't shake the idea that you dread something—"

"I am quite certain," she interrupted. "I hope you won't worry about me." Years of living under her father's expectations of serenity and composure were coming to her aid now. Her voice was clear and even, and she was able to hold herself with calm poise. And she meant what she said: she *didn't* want him to worry about her, because there was nothing he could do to help her anyway.

"Well. If you are satisfied..." He didn't sound convinced but he led her into the yard. "I'll see to your ticket."

That would be another debt she owed him, but she could repay this one. Samantha had memorized the street and number of his lodging, and hoped she could contrive a way to send a token of thanks along with the repaid fare.

But no sooner had they stepped through the gate into the bustling coaching yard than her poise splintered. Directly across from them, looking like a thundercloud, stood her father, tapping his whip against his boot in obvious impatience. A servant led away his sweating horse, and the earl snapped at another groom as he strode toward the open door of the inn.

Samantha's feet rooted to the ground, dragging Lord George to a halt beside her. He looked at her in question, but she couldn't speak. She had braced herself for a scene when she returned home. There was a slender chance the earl would not have heard of her disappearance, but Samantha was resigned to suffering for that as well. What she hadn't prepared for was the chance that her father would be *here,* where Lord George would be witness to her humiliation. Even worse, he would discover exactly who she was, and if her father did indeed marry her to Lord Philip, he would know why she'd run away.

"Samantha?" Lord George covered her hand with his. "What's wrong?"

She stared at him, her heart plummeting. There would be a scene, at either his or her father's instigation. Lord George had saved her from ruffians with reckless disregard for his own safety; any man who plunged into the Thames to save a strange woman would be likely to commit other foolhardy acts of gallantry. He might protest her father hauling her off in a fury. Few insults set off the earl's temper like being questioned in public. Not only would his anger at her be doubled, he would lash out at Lord George. And when Stratford learned it was Rowland's son…

Without conscious thought she took a step backward, and then another. Lord George said something, his forehead creased with concern, but she couldn't understand it. Her eyes prickled with tears of shame and guilt and fear. She could bear it all if only he didn't have to see…

Her father emerged from the inn, his face set in the cold, harsh lines she knew too well, and her nerve broke. She threw off Lord George's hand and spun on her heel, walking away as fast as her legs would take her. She gripped her hands in fists at her sides, not caring where she went. If someone kidnapped her again, she would willingly abandon herself to whatever they inflicted upon her.

An arm went around her waist. "The coach runs to Richmond every day," said Lord George. "There's no need to rush aboard. Shall we walk?" Since she was still charging forward, he didn't wait for an answer. "Would you like to see the park, my lady?" He grinned, but Samantha couldn't look at him. "Right," he said after a moment. "A good walk doesn't need conversation. This way."

By the time they reached Charing Cross, her shins burned and her feet felt disconnected from her body. Her pace slowed, and, after a quick glance, Lord George dropped his arm from her waist. Samantha realized it had been there all along, holding her up and helping shield her from passersby. He wrapped her hand around his arm, and she didn't protest.

They walked at a slower pace for some time. She was grateful he didn't speak. Gradually her heart stopped pounding so painfully hard, and the cold bitter truth of her situation lay before her.

She had no money, and no clothing beyond the stained and mended dress she wore.

She couldn't turn to Benedict.

She had nowhere to go but home, to her father.

She saw no way to ameliorate his fury at what she had done, not just by stealing and keeping it secret for seven years, but now running away.

She would be fortunate if her father didn't find someone worse than Lord Philip.

Samantha slipped her hand off Lord George's arm. "I'm sorry," she said in a low voice.

"For what?"

"I shouldn't have taken advantage of your hospitality last night. I should have dried myself off and gone on my way at once."

"Gone where?"

"To—it doesn't matter."

"It does to me." Now he stopped, but his mild tone didn't change. "I don't just save young ladies from kidnappers or fish them out of the Thames without forming some concern for them."

She forced an unhappy smile. "In this case you should."

For a long moment he regarded her with thoughtful eyes. "What did you see at the coaching inn that frightened you?"

"Nothing."

"*Whom* did you see?"

She flushed; he knew. "It doesn't matter."

He sighed and took hold of her arm, leading her to a nearby bench. "I have one thing to say, Perdita, and I hope you'll believe me. I want to help you. If you don't want my help, you can refuse it, but please don't lie to me. It only makes me imagine the worst, and as my mother could warn you, I have a terrifyingly active imagination." He pulled a handkerchief from his pocket and held it out. Samantha hadn't even realized her eyes were wet until then.

"Very well." She dabbed at her eyes, and discreetly blew her nose. "You were right, I don't wish to go home. I did something terrible. I—I lied to my father and schemed to help someone he despised. It was years ago but I only recently confessed, and he is very displeased."

"And you're afraid of being punished?" His voice was so warm and sympathetic.

Samantha shook her head. "I knew I would be punished. I didn't know how. He said he would arrange a marriage for me…" The image of Lord Philip, handsome and vicious, swam before her eyes. She folded the handkerchief for a fresh swipe across her face.

"To someone you don't know?"

"I know him," she whispered. "He is cruel. More than one person thinks he's mad. His family connections would make him a splendid match but no lady even wants to dance with him. And my father—my father—"

Lord George's expression had grown darker throughout her halting explanation. "You ran away to avoid the marriage."

"I know someone in London… I thought that person might help me think of a way to dissuade my father…" A bitter laugh escaped her. "That was foolish, though, and I panicked when I saw the coach and thought of facing him."

"Then you shall not go back." He caught her hand and pressed it between his two. "Not until you have thought of a way to change his mind. No woman should be forced into a marriage she fears."

"I don't have anywhere to stay," she told him miserably. "I cannot go to…the person I thought might help me."

"You'll stay at Mrs. Willis's," he said at once.

"My rooms are yours for as long as you need them."

She was already shaking her head. "I can't…"

"Well." He smiled boyishly. "You could repay me." Alarm must have flickered over her face, for he hurried to add, "By letting me sketch you. Your face would be just right in my next work."

"The shipwreck? Her face is turned away…"

"Not that rubbish." He flicked away mention of a work of art with a quick motion of his fingers. "The better painting I'm planning. Your face will be on a young woman in church, nothing immodest. I'll show you a sketch before you make an answer." Without waiting for a reply, he rummaged in his pockets, pulling out a scrap of coarse paper and a charcoal pencil, like the one he had used to draw the skunk earlier. "I was thinking of a young woman, on her knees in supplication at the altar," he said, flattening the paper on his knee and beginning to sketch. "Other figures in the church are engaged in petty arguments or merely there to sightsee, but she alone evinces real faith and hope."

Samantha watched the scene blossom under his pencil. She imagined sitting in his studio as he drew her face. It was tempting, so tempting, but… "I don't think it would be wise to let my likeness be painted."

"No one will recognize you. It will be quite small, I promise to obscure your features. But…" His gaze roved over her face, fascinated and eager. "You're exactly the sort of model I hoped to find. I would consider it more than ample repayment for anything I've done for you."

This time Samantha didn't bother contemplating what her father would think. She was so far beyond the pale, it hardly mattered. Perhaps she would never go home, and would simply flit about the shadows of London. At the moment it sounded far more appealing than anything that required her to face the earl.

She took a deep breath. "Lord George—"

"Gray," he said. "Please."

Somehow that felt more intimate than calling him by his proper title. "Gray," she said softly. "Thank you. I accept."

CHAPTER SEVEN

Gray knew Mrs. Willis would extract a pound of flesh—in pounds sterling—for his wild offer to Samantha. His landlady would put the most rapacious moneylender to shame. He'd taken the rooms in her house because of the excellent light in the large topmost room, which made an ideal studio, and because it was very convenient to the Strand, which bustled with artistic life and supply shops. His apartments on the floor below, nothing more than a bedroom and a sitting room, were functional, and his rent included dinner if he wished it. It was the perfect situation for a bachelor artist, but now he'd gone and upset the whole arrangement by promising indefinite shelter to a well-born young woman of nebulous history.

He didn't care. He could no more turn out Samantha than he could give up painting. The stark, frozen look on her face when she'd turned and walked out of the coaching yard had shocked him and made him want to commit assault on the person who had so terrified her. Not that he had any idea who that was; he'd gone after her the moment she turned, and had snatched only a quick searching glance back at the busy yard. It could have been any of a dozen people, but it didn't really matter.

Her story only confirmed his suspicion. By now Gray had put together enough to make him feel very protective toward her. She was a lady, groomed to make an advantageous match; the thought of marrying a man she didn't know well was probably not foreign to her, and yet she'd run away, and then lost her nerve even after declaring she was ready to go home and face it. He could think of a few so-called eligible gentlemen who fit her description of cruel and mad, but he had a harder time thinking of a peer, or even a gentleman, who would willingly wed a daughter to any of them. Perhaps her father was banking on a wealthy husband for her, to save his own fortunes. Gray made a mental note to ask his mother if she knew anyone near Richmond who fit that description.

Back in Stanhope Street, he left Samantha in the parlor and went directly to find Mrs. Willis. It was always best to catch her off guard; she'd extort her price, but on no account was she going to refuse.

It took some doing, with several mentions of Samantha's genteel background and appeals to Mrs. Willis's sense of Christian charity, but in the end she agreed Samantha could stay for an extra guinea a week. Since that was far more than Gray's own rent, he argued successfully that it would include both breakfast and dinner every day, so Samantha wouldn't need to leave the house if she didn't want to, and for Mrs. Willis to procure suitable clothing for his guest.

He was thankful, however, that it was nearly quarter day when his father would pay his allowance. He'd spent liberally on canvases and paints recently, and this was going to cost him dearly. Then he dismissed the thought of money and went to tell Samantha.

"All settled," he said, letting himself into the

parlor.

She smiled nervously. "Thank you. I don't know what I'll do with myself…"

"There's no pianoforte, but you could draw to your heart's delight." He hesitated, then threw caution to the wind. "You could also help in the studio, if you've a mind to do it. I have no catalog of my work, and it would be helpful to have one."

Her face brightened, and he thought he'd never seen anyone so lovely. Her eyes glowed like polished jade, and her smile did terrible things to Gray's sense of honor. "I would be delighted," she said shyly.

"Excellent!" Even though he'd never spent two minutes worrying about a catalog of his paintings, Gray beamed as if she'd just solved his greatest worry in life. "I may never want you to leave, if you make yourself that useful."

A flush of color came into her cheeks and she gave him a glance that brimmed with teasing. "Perhaps I'll make a terrible mess of it. You may lock me out after the first day."

Gray scoffed. "Impossible. I did say I haven't got any catalog right now, didn't I? You can't do worse than that."

Now her eyes sparkled, and she lifted her chin, still smiling, as if taking on a challenge. "I'll do my best."

Life in Stanhope Street was nothing like life at Stratford Court. Mrs. Willis was as keen-eyed as the housekeeper in Richmond, but far more voluble. Her voice rang up and down the stairs of the neat little house from morning till night as she bickered with the cook, who only came in the afternoons; chattered with the handful of other ladies who came to gossip under the guise of being a ladies' sewing society; and chastised Jenny for a variety of sins, from leaving a dust rag in sight to forgetting to black the grates in her sitting room. She seemed to keep a keen ear out for the sound of Gray's footsteps, which would always send her running after him, calling out for him to stop a moment. Samantha soon understood why he closed himself into his studio most days, even going so far as to post a notice on the door at one point: *Silence requested*.

Of course she was also aware that her

presence had evicted him from his apartment and left him nowhere to go but the painting studio. Within an hour of telling her she could stay as long as she pleased, he had packed all his possessions and carted them up the stairs, leaving the bedroom and sitting room to her. Stealing wildly curious glances at her the whole while, Jenny gave the apartment a cursory cleaning, and from them on Samantha was part of the household.

The next day Mrs. Willis brought in a pair of dresses, plainer and sturdier than anything in her wardrobe at home, and presented them proudly to her. Feeling as though she had entered a very strange dream, Samantha tried them both on, for it was clear she couldn't wear her frock of glazed pink muslin much longer. Even washed and mended it was beginning to look shabby, and her maid at home would be aghast if she saw it.

"Well, it's too long, but Jenny can take that up," fussed Mrs. Willis over the striped blue dress. The other one, pale yellow with green flowers, needed to be taken in as well, so soon Jenny came in with a box of sewing supplies.

"Thank you for helping me," Samantha told her.

"'Tis my pleasure," said Jenny frankly, pinning up the hem where Mrs. Willis had marked it. "Mending's a vast deal better than blacking grates, and I forgot to do the one in Aunt Tansy's sitting room again." She said the last in a whisper. "As if it needs blacking every day! I'm sure she only puts me to it so I won't have a moment to m'self. 'Idleness is wickedness,'" she said, imitating her aunt's breathy manner of speaking. "As if I would know! Never a pause from morning until night." She shook her head and bit off a length of thread.

"I could help," Samantha offered after a few minutes. She'd only done embroidery, never stitching her own clothing, but Jenny was sewing a rather lackadaisical seam, and she was sure she could do better than that.

"If'n you want." The girl handed over the blue dress, the needle still dangling from the thread.

Samantha spread it over her lap and set to work. A creak overhead made her look up, but no other sound came from the studio upstairs. Gray hadn't appeared all day, and she didn't have the nerve to knock and interrupt him.

"So it is true you've run away from home to avoid a terrible marriage?"

She flinched at Jenny's bold, eager question. "What makes you think that?"

"I overheard Aunt Tansy tellin' Mrs. Johnson who lives next door. Everyone'll be quite rabid to know all about you, miss." Jenny's eyes shone as she sat forward. "Is't true?"

Samantha concentrated on her stitches. Did everyone know? "Something like it."

"I knew it," breathed the girl in excitement. "It's just like *The Romance of the Forest*! Is he very evil, the man you're supposed to marry?"

Instinctively Samantha began to deny it, thought again of Lord Philip shooting out a horse's legs one by one, and said nothing.

"And Lord George saved you from him." Jenny sighed happily. "Right noble, don't you think?"

Samantha gave her a stern glance. "He's been very kind to me, particularly for being a stranger."

"Aye, he's a kind one," Jenny agreed. "He gave me a crown for that bonnet you took the other day, even though it were two years old and not even my best. He told me not to tell Aunt Tansy, for she'd want half." She looked up. "Is that how it works with gentry? You marry whosomever your pa chooses?"

Samantha didn't know how it was in other families, but in hers… "Yes."

"Can't you refuse?" Jenny's eyebrows went up at Samantha's quick shake of the head. "Blimey. What if you fancy another gent? If'n you run off with someone else, your pa couldn't make you marry the other one."

Samantha almost smiled at the girl's eager embrace of the idea—which had occurred to her, more than once. Unfortunately she didn't *fancy another gent,* nor even know one who would consider defying the Earl of Stratford to elope with her. "A dramatic solution."

The girl shrugged. "Beddin' someone else would do near the same, aye?"

Now Samantha was shocked. "Jenny! Mrs. Willis would be appalled."

Jenny rolled her eyes. "Aunt Tansy's appalled by everythin' I do and say; 't'ain't hard to rile her temper. Besides…" She slid a little closer, her dark eyes shining. "Ain't you thought of it?"

Samantha thought her eyes must be about to fall from her head. How on earth could this girl—who couldn't be more than fifteen or sixteen—talk about such things? "Certainly not!" she whispered indignantly.

"Not even with yon gentleman?" Jenny grinned, her eyes flickering upward toward the studio. "He admires you something fierce, he does. Not even a kiss?"

"No!"

Jenny tipped her head back, a knowing look creeping over her face. "Oh, on account o' being a proper lady? My mum says proper ladies don't know aught about men and bedding until they marry. Is't true?"

The color in her cheeks was probably answer enough, but Samantha still added a repressive, "Yes."

"And you be not curious? He's a right handsome lad, that Lord George." Jenny seemed more perplexed than anything, as if she couldn't understand how anyone could be immune to Gray's appeal. "If'n he tried to kiss me, I'd let him."

She made a horrified sound before she could stop herself. "Has he—?"

Jenny made a face. "Not a bit. Nor would Aunt Tansy allow it anyway. She'd scour my hide if she caught me smiling at him, she'd never get another tenant to pay like he does… But *you*," she exclaimed with relish. "You're a lady, and he's a gent. 'T'ain't wrong for you to look at him."

"Jenny," said Samantha, breathing hard as she tried to fend off the thought of Gray kissing her, "you shouldn't speak so. It's immodest and indelicate."

The girl snickered. "Immodest! You ought to read *Fifty Ways*. Lady Constance could open your eyes, she could." She leaned forward. "You ain't read it, 'ave you? Fiendishly scandalous. You don't look the scandalous type of lady."

"No," said Samantha, but not without a small hesitation. Just being here was a scandal for her, but she had a feeling Jenny meant

121

something far more wicked. Lucy Walgrave had whispered about something called *50 Ways to Sin* once, but Samantha had never dared ask more.

"You must!" Jenny bounded out of her chair, mending forgotten. "I'll fetch it."

Still blushing furiously, Samantha bent her head over the dress. She had broken so many rules of decency already, it could hardly matter if she breached one more.

And there was one point of truth in Jenny's chatter. Bedding someone would ruin her irreparably as a bride, for Lord Philip or anyone of his class.

She ducked her head, unable to believe such thoughts were running through her mind. She was a lady, raised properly and respectably. Her sole duty in life was to marry well and bear children of unimpeachable lineage. Lord Philip might be mad and dangerous, but he was from the same society, and his father was well known for his pride. It was highly likely neither of them would want her if she weren't a virgin still...

"Here!" Jenny slipped back into the room, startling her so badly she sent the needle right into her finger. "Deliciously wicked," the maid whispered in excitement. "Oh Lor', how I wish I could do half the things!"

"What is it?" Pressing her wounded finger with her thumb, Samantha took the simple pamphlet.

"You'll know soon enough." Looking superior, Jenny retrieved her mending and went back to work.

With a worried look at the door, Samantha slowly set down the dress and opened the pamphlet. The very first paragraph made her eyes widen. "Jenny! This is indecent!"

"O' course it is! I overheard Aunt Tansy and Mrs. Barber talking about it over their tea one day. Nipped out as soon as I could to find it myself. Read on, it gets better," she urged. "That's the first one, but I got most of 'em collected, you can borrow as many as you like."

She should put the wicked thing away, and yet her eyes strayed back to the pamphlet. Before she knew it, she had reached the end; it was only a few pages long, though so full of shocking things it made her face burn and her skin feel tight. Good heavens. She wasn't completely ignorant of how a man bedded a woman, but she'd never heard it described this way, as if the woman might enjoy it, even crave it. For a moment she pictured herself lying back, reaching for a lover, her body burning for his touch, and the lover who loomed over her, eyes dark with hunger, hands cupping her face, touching her body….

…Was Lord George Churchill-Gray.

Samantha slapped the pamphlet closed and thrust it back at Jenny. "Very imaginative," she managed to choke out.

Jenny giggled again, sliding the story into her apron pocket. "D' you want more?"

"No!"

"No?" The girl looked astonished. "There's a powerful one, where she takes a gentleman into the cloakroom at the theater, and the newest story is even better—a gent ties her to the bed with scarlet ribbons, oh my, that one…"

Samantha sat like a statue, trying and failing to divert her mind from the idea. Tied down? How was that pleasurable? Lord George's laughing eyes kept drifting across her mind, and a shudder went through her as she recalled the feel of his arms around her, holding her easily against his chest; of his arm about her waist, cradling her protectively against him; of his fingers on her face, swearing he would help her avoid whatever had sent her running... She cleared her throat. "Well..."

Jenny looked up, a grin lurking on her lips.

"Perhaps one more," Samantha whispered, and knew that this was how the serpent had led Eve astray.

CHAPTER EIGHT

Gray soon became convinced that saving Samantha was the cleverest thing he'd done in years.

It was true that he had to sleep on the ridiculous chaise in the studio, which could in no way be called comfortable. All his possessions were also jumbled in a heap in the corner of the studio, in danger of being spattered with paint and mineral spirits. And Mrs. Willis now regarded it as her right to speak to him each and every day about something or other, despite the extortionate rent he was paying and his extensive efforts to avoid her.

But every time he felt a pang for the way things used to be, he would catch sight of Samantha, and his heart would give a little sigh of delight. For all that he knew she was a lady and a guest at the moment, she offered to help around the house; he'd seen her sewing and mending, and every time the landlady chased him down, Mrs. Willis assured him she was faultlessly polite and charming. The thought of her being given to a man who terrified her made him feel capable of murder.

The crowning moment of victory, though, came when Samantha knocked on the studio door. "Mrs. Willis has gone out," she said as soon as he opened it. "And Jenny. No sooner did Mrs. Willis leave than she shot out the back of the house, calling back something about an errand. If you would like me to begin your catalog, I am ready."

"At last, my prayers answered." He threw open the door and extended his arm. "Please come in, my lady."

He caught a whiff of roses as she passed. It was the same scent as Mrs. Willis's soap, but somehow it smelled far more alluring on Samantha than on his landlady. "Let me get you some ink and a pen... I've never done a catalog but I'm sure there's something suitable lying about..." He rummaged around and produced a notebook, and a moment later a sharpened pencil. "This will serve for now."

He didn't really care much for having a catalog. Every picture he had ever crafted existed in minute detail in his memory. But he was keenly interested in finding something that would excuse Samantha spending hours near him, and if he ended up with a list of his paintings in her handwriting, so much the better.

She accepted the book and pencil, her brow clear and untroubled. "I'm sure it will. I promise to be as quiet as I can, to avoid interrupting your work."

"Right." He retreated to his canvas, nudging the easel so he could more easily spy around the side and see her. "I hope you have some fondness for landscapes."

"Yes." She was taking stock of the canvases stacked around the room. "Have you got a measuring tape?"

"Oh—yes." He scrambled to find it, tucking away another interesting fact. She knew to record the dimensions of a painting. She thanked him with a bright smile, and he felt it like a mule kick to the chest. He didn't know her name, her family, her situation, and she had already admitted she was defying her father, who was determined to marry her to a cruel and dangerous man; all these factors should persuade him to keep her at a very wary distance, and yet he had the growing feeling that he would end up doing just the opposite.

She worked quietly, and with some effort Gray turned his attention back to the canvas in front of him. The hurricane had been set aside; the dark-haired woman who had escaped disaster no longer interested him. He had already sketched in the broad strokes of the soaring cathedral. Once inspiration struck, he was capable of working exhausting hours, unable to think of food or sleep. For a while he worked at filling in the figures of the background: the gossiping women in fashionable gowns, the dozing gentleman with his dog half-hidden under his feet, the sanctimonious curate fawning over the red-faced nobleman commanding his attention. Only at the center did he leave a blank spot, for the girl.

After several hours of peace, Gray dared a
covert glance around the canvas. Samantha had
a small portrait on the second easel. He watched
as she carefully measured it, noted the
dimensions, and kept writing.

And writing. And writing some more. What
was she writing?

"Coming on all right?" he asked.

She looked up, startled. Her eyes were as
green as the Irish Sea near Kirkwood. "Yes.
Would you like to see? I should have asked if
you had any particular requirements."

"Of course." He wiped his hands and strode
across the room, telling himself it was purely to
see what she'd done, and not simply to stand
next to her. She handed him the book, and it
took him a moment to register anything about
it. Wisps of blond hair had come loose from the
braided knot at her nape and curled around her
neck. Even in a fairly dowdy blue dress she was
beautiful.

"Will it do?" she asked as he stared at her.

Gray snapped his gaze down to the
notebook. "Yes," he said automatically, and
then he started to really read it. It was more

than adequate, to his surprise. He turned the page, and saw the same meticulous care applied to every picture. She had described them, noted the dimensions, the medium, and questions: *year? subject? companion pieces?* "It's excellent," he murmured.

Her face glowed. "I'm so glad. I didn't wish to disturb you to ask titles, but I left a place for them."

"I haven't got titles for most," he said absently. She had recorded everything so that he could cut the paper into slips, one for each painting, and pin them on the back as labels.

"Once it's complete, if you fill in the years of creation and other missing information, I'll create a master list in chronological order for you to keep. It will help as you send pieces to dealers and exhibitions, for you can record where each painting was sent and who purchased it."

"How did you know to do it this way?" Gray asked, still marveling at her notes. "This is exactly what I need. How did you know?"

He looked up in time to see the flash of alarm in her face, as if he'd just discovered something distasteful about her. Then she laughed a little. "Oh—I presumed… Did I do it well, then?"

"Beautifully." Another useful fact: she knew what sort of records art dealers kept. "But it's not complete." He held out the book. "There are no illustrations."

Her expression was perfectly blank, then she burst out laughing. "Those don't belong in a catalog!"

"In my catalog they do." He retrieved the pencil and gave it to her. "I like dogs and horses."

"Horses are impossible!" But she took the pencil, her face still flushed with laughter.

Gray grinned. "Hedgehogs. Squirrels. Deer and snakes and elephants."

She gave him a stern glance. Irrationally buoyed, he went back to his canvas.

It astonished him that he could work with her in the room, but somehow he did. Mrs. Willis, well used to his painting habits, made only a token fuss about Samantha working in the studio with him, and soon his daily routine seemed to revolve around her arrival. Normally he liked quiet while he painted, as the scene came to vivid life, complete with sound, in his head. But Samantha's presence, far from disturbing him, seemed to improve his focus. Everything came off his brush the right way, and inspiration abounded. He added a mouse to the corner, stealing crumbs from the hem of the curate's robes. The only thing he didn't paint a single stroke of was the girl at the center of the piece. He was waiting for her.

It never escaped his mind that these days with Samantha would end. Every time he stole a glimpse of her bent over another picture, he felt a growing need to find some happy solution to her problem. A solution that would allow her to return home without fear. A solution that would permit her to find a more acceptable husband, one she would never run from in terror. One who would appreciate what a beauty she was, and how kind she was, and one who knew how to make her eyes light up with mischief and delight.

He tried very hard not to let his thoughts drift too far down that path. Gray had nothing against matrimony—he was twenty-seven, after all, and certainly didn't want to grow old alone—but he feared he would make a poor husband right now. What sort of wife would tolerate a husband who disappeared into a painting studio for hours, even days, at a time? What woman would overlook the smell of mineral spirits and oil paints? Samantha did, but only because she was hiding from something even worse. Which was not to say he enjoyed the thought of her married to someone else. And if he let himself think of another man holding her close and kissing her, nuzzling her neck until she laughed and let her eyes drop closed as the fellow laid her back and unbuttoned her dress to savor her lovely breasts... He blotted the canvas in a way that made him swear out loud.

All in all, Gray thought the best choice was to find an argument that would dissuade her father from his course. What she chose to do after that would be her decision entirely.

Samantha knew the idyll could not last forever.

The question of her future hovered over her, like the grim and dour portrait of some Stratford ancestor that used to hang in the parlor where she had her dance lessons. She could almost feel that long-dead earl glaring down on her, as he had done on her lessons: *shame,* he seemed to whisper in disdain. She was a shame to the illustrious Stratford family, a thief and a liar and now a runaway.

Despite many hours spent agonizing over it, she hadn't formulated a promising plan. More than ever she wished she had some way to speak to Benedict, but with each day that slipped away, it seemed harder and harder. Mindful of her father's presence in London, she tried to avoid leaving the house, although if Gray invited her to walk around the corner to purchase more paint, she found it hard to refuse. As long as she was with him, she felt safe.

But Samantha knew he must be thinking about her situation, too, and was not surprised when he asked, after a few days of work on his catalog, "What did you do that angered your father?"

135

She took a moment to frame her answer. "I tried to help someone I was very fond of." How long ago it felt, that she'd fancied herself in love with Sebastian. "He was a dear friend of my brother's and his family had suffered terrible misfortunes. I stole some money from my father and gave it to my friend, hoping it would help him."

"Did it?"

She sighed bitterly. "It made things worse. My father thought *he* had stolen the money, and called him a thief."

"And your father never suspected you?"

She shook her head. Stratford had been perfectly pleased to think Sebastian Vane was the thief. That was the only reason she could think of for why he had never investigated the matter further.

"But you told him," Gray went on slowly. "And he was angry. Not shocking, I suppose."

"What would your father do?" she asked. "If he discovered you had lied to him."

"If! You speak as though it never happened." He grinned. "It depended on the lie. If I hadn't done my lessons, I had to do them twice, under his eye. If I fought with my brothers, he made me apologize to my mother for not heeding her instruction on proper gentlemanly deportment. She had a way of looking so disappointed, I dreaded that more than doing the Latin twice."

She smiled wistfully.

"Does he know this fellow is cruel?"

Gray's voice made her start. She looked up to see him watching her. Today his long hair was tied back with a bit of string, and it made his dark eyes all the more piercing.

"The fellow your father would like you to marry," he added in a gentle voice.

Samantha looked away. "Yes." She could feel his gaze on her still.

"I tried to think what my father would do if he had the power to arrange his children's marriages at whim. Tom in particular gives him fits, and if Father could find a woman to settle him, he would move heaven and earth to get her into a church. But I can't imagine he would want someone Tom didn't fancy in the slightest."

"It's different with daughters," Samantha

137

said in a low voice.

"I thought of that, too," Gray said, unruffled. "My conclusion there is that he'd put Rowland to rack and ruin before he gave a daughter of his to any but the most highly approved man in England. And then I suspect he'd keep his eye on the fellow all the rest of his days, to be sure his daughter was happy."

Unconsciously her fingers tightened on the pencil. Slowly she drew a curved line in the margin, where he had told her he wanted illustration. "But you don't know... He has no daughter, let alone one who lied to him and stole from him..."

"I pictured a younger version of my mother. The one time my father raised a hand to any of us boys was the time Rob—very ill-advisedly—threw off her hand and shouted at her. He thought he was too old to be scolded about his manners, and it made her weep. Father took him by the throat and pinned him up against the wall until Rob nearly soiled himself, and after that none of us dared say a smart word to our mother."

Samantha drew another curve, opposite the

first, then two tiny triangles. "He's not like my father."

"I gathered." Gray was quiet for several minutes. Samantha's fingers kept working, feathering lines along the lower curve, adding eyes and whiskers. "Are you of age?"

She dropped the pencil, then blushed furiously at the question. "Yes."

"Then you don't need his permission to marry."

Just as Jenny had suggested: *If'n you run off with someone else, your pa couldn't make you marry the other one.* Samantha retrieved the pencil and finished her doodle with sharp, angry strokes. The frightened little fox gazed off the page at her, tucked under a concealing hedge. All well and good for Jenny, who was only fifteen, and Gray, who was a man, to say she could solve her problem by marrying someone else. As if there was anyone she could possibly marry…

She looked up and caught Gray's eyes again. No longer painting, he stood watching her with his arms folded, his face serious. And just like that, Jenny's other suggestion welled up in her mind. If she seduced Gray, like that wicked

Lady Constance in the pamphlet, she'd be ruined as a bride for the Marquess of Dorre's son, as surely as if she eloped with someone else.

Just as quickly as the thought came to her, Samantha recoiled from it. "What are you saying?" she snapped. She stood up and dropped the catalog on the chair. "That I should make a hasty marriage, because anyone would be better than Lord Ph—?"

"No!" he said violently, crossing the room in three steps. "I meant that if you had another suitor, more acceptable to you, he could be prompted to save you from…" His words trailed off as first one, then a half dozen tears slid down her cheeks. "Samantha…"

"There's no one else," she choked. "No other suitor—I was never allowed to have any. None of them suited Father, you see? There may not be a man in England who would marry me, and certainly none who could be called upon to conduct an illicit courtship in extreme haste—"

He pushed a handkerchief into her hand. "I daresay there's a hundred men in London who would leap at the chance to court you, if offered. Not that I suggested that."

"It would be a stupid proposal, if you did," she raged on, unable to stop the tears. She was twenty-three, sheltered and caged by her gilded existence, without a suitor of any kind, and helpless to save herself. She didn't even have a friend to unburden herself to but had to run away and lose herself among strangers. "You should know that."

"Because…?"

"Because I can't just marry any man I please!"

"And why not, if you're of age?"

She dragged the handkerchief over her eyes once more and put it down. "Without a likely candidate, it hardly matters. I know—I've known all along—that I have to go back eventually. Perhaps if I stay away long enough, it will disrupt the match he's arranged. Then it won't matter, and I'll spend the rest of my life at home, taking care to stay out of his sight—"

Her despondent diatribe was cut short when Gray tipped up her chin and kissed her. Samantha inhaled in shock, but almost instantly relaxed. His lips were soft and warm against hers. She'd never been kissed before and it was...lovely. Tentatively she responded. His hands cupped her jaw, holding her, and when she made a murmur of astonishment, his tongue traced her lips in suggestion.

It made her think of some of the more wicked things in *50 Ways to Sin*. Somehow she'd managed to borrow a great many more than two from Jenny. It seemed to have catapulted Samantha headlong from innocent girl to a woman, whose longings and feelings suddenly felt normal instead of shamefully indecent. She had imagined lovemaking as something to be endured as her duty to a husband; it was the only way to provide an heir and therefore she must resign herself to it. But Constance reveled in it and abruptly Samantha knew why. Just kissing Gray was wonderful. Perhaps she too would become a notorious woman and live a decadent and independent life... She opened her mouth to his questing tongue, and promptly forgot everything else.

She didn't know how long the kiss lasted, but she felt breathless and disoriented when it ended, and at the same time she hoped he'd kiss her again.

"Never say there's not a man in England who would marry you," Gray murmured. His hands moved over her shoulders, gliding softly down her back.

Samantha clung to him. Kissing her wasn't the same as wanting to marry her, but she had a feeling Gray would be more than happy to carry her over to the chaise and show her the sorts of pleasure Lady Constance wrote of. His muscles were tense and hard beneath her hands, his breathing ragged as he held her close.

And for the first time in her life, Samantha felt bold and daring enough to do it. What would it cost her that she hadn't already lost? She had lived her whole life knowing she would marry the man her father chose, a man who might well not want her. This could be her only chance to have a man who pleased *her*...

Feeling reckless, she turned her head and pressed her lips against Gray's jaw. The scratch of stubble made her shiver; he felt so masculine, so different, and a shiver of excitement went through her. Her arm slid around his neck and she went up on her toes to brush her lips against his.

Gray's arms tightened around her, pulling her against him. "If you kiss me that way, you're asking for trouble," he whispered, his voice a low rumble in his chest.

"What kind of trouble?" Samantha was shocked by the breathless, eager tone of her voice. And yet she was also thrilled by the feel of him against her.

For answer he kissed her back, his fingers plowing into her hair and his mouth harder, demanding. Her lips parted in astonishment, and his tongue swept in, tasting her. He took two steps forward and her back hit the wall. Gray leaned into her, pressing their bodies together from shoulder to hip, and his knee pushed between her legs.

Samantha gasped, and he groaned, rocking back and forth ever-so-slightly. His thigh rose between hers until it nestled against her intimately—the place Lady Constance called her quim—and instead of feeling invasive it felt so *right* she rubbed against him.

With a start Gray broke the kiss. His eyes

were almost black, and his chest heaved. He stared at her for a moment, his brows drawn together, then he took a big step back even though his hands remained on her, holding her to the wall. "Trouble," he rasped. "The sort of trouble you don't need." Gingerly, as if afraid she'd fall over, he released her.

She wrapped her arms around her waist, realizing her nipples were standing firm and hard under her dress. Gray looked as rattled as she felt, so she half turned away, unsure what to say. "Thank you."

"Thank—?" He gave a bark of rueful laughter and retreated another step. "You should slap my face."

"No." She looked up at him. "I liked it."

His pained smile faded. He looked at her for a long, searching moment. "So did I."

Even though she knew it was wrong, his admission sparked a glow inside her. She ducked her head so he couldn't see her tiny smile of delight. Her first real kiss, more thrilling and stirring than she had ever expected.

"Samantha." When she looked up, Gray looked more in control of himself again. "I promised you would not have to go home. I meant it."

"I have nowhere else—"

"You will," he cut off her protest. "Give me time and I will have a safe, respectable place for you to stay as long as you wish, and your father will not be able to touch you. Will you trust me?"

She should politely refuse, but…that kiss. "Yes," she whispered. "I do."

CHAPTER NINE

By now Gray sensed he had enough information to discover Samantha's identity, which perversely meant he no longer wanted to know. He knew only one person who would be willing to help Samantha with no questions asked, and who possessed both the social cachet and personal courage to stare down anyone, even a peer of the realm, who might want to drag her away. Unfortunately, that person was not in London at the moment, a minor complication Gray set about solving at once. He sent off a letter express, and went back to his studio. The answer to his letter, when it came, would mean the end of Samantha's time in Stanhope Street, and his fingers still burned to draw her.

He posed her carefully, mindful of his

promise that the figure would be respectful, on her knees as if in prayer. "Raise your chin an inch," he directed, "and your hands."

She obeyed, clasping her hands directly in front of her breasts. Gray wasn't above stealing a quick look. He planned to paint the girl in his cathedral in a shabby coat, but it was much too warm to ask Samantha to pose in one. Or so he told himself as his gaze lingered on the swell of her flesh above the dress bodice.

"Like this?" she asked, her own eyes trained on the far side of the room.

He jerked his eyes down to the sketch pad on his knee. "Yes." She was beautiful—perfect, really—her expression sweet with devotion and hope. His pencil moved over the paper lightly, trying to catch the exact curve of her cheek and angle of her nose. Her ear, just visible beneath the coil of her hair. The slope of her neck. The expression in her eyes. He drew one sketch, then another, then another, racing to capture the image, stamped in her likeness, on paper.

"That's enough for now," he said, belatedly realizing how long she'd held the pose.

With a sigh of relief she lowered her hands

and rolled her head. "Were you able to get a good sketch?"

"Oh yes." He spread out the studies, rough and preliminary though they were. There would be more, but now her face was engraved on his memory, every curve and line and shade of color. He did not show her the sketches he had already drawn, of her measuring canvases or bent over her mending. He wanted to record everything about her against the day she left.

He had told himself in no uncertain terms that he was not going to kiss her again, nor hold her again, nor even offer her his arm again. She felt so good against him, so tempting and willing, he didn't trust himself to stop. He needed to remember he was a gentleman, able to resist such desires. To that end he began taking more care with his toilet, making sure to shave every morning and wearing proper clothes instead of his usual slapdash painting outfits. Surely a waistcoat would be a tactile sign of honor, proof that he knew his place and—more importantly—hers.

And yet... He wasn't sure it worked. Every day he found himself more and more eager for her to come up to the studio. Just the sound of her footsteps on the stairs made his heart leap. When she came in, her blond curls pinned neatly up and a bright smile on her face, it felt as if the day grew brighter. He even painted better when she was there; his cathedral painting was flowing like nothing ever had before.

Samantha was examining the sketches. "Do I really look like this?"

"No," he said. "You're far lovelier."

She darted a glance at him.

"It's true." He lifted one shoulder. "I wish I were a better artist, to capture you accurately."

"Oh no!" She put her hand on his wrist. "You're a splendid artist. I… I didn't recognize myself."

"Why not?"

Samantha ran one finger over a sketch of her face. "I look happy," she said softly. "Hopeful."

"How do you feel?" he asked after a moment of shock.

She looked up at him. "The same."

A fierce satisfaction surged in his breast.

"I'm relieved to hear that! Here I put you to work, measuring a pile of paintings and cataloging them… Quite a host, eh?"

"Not at all!" She blushed. "You've given me far more help than I've given you."

He waved it away, but it nudged the awkward question of her future back into view. "What do you hope for?" he asked on impulse.

Her face grew pensive. "To go to the theater whenever I wish. To dance a reel in full view of society. To walk or ride in the park and not care who sees me laughing. Simple things, really."

"But delightful."

"I want to see Venice," she said, her tone growing more determined. "And the mountains of Switzerland. Even the Lake District. I've never been away from Richmond and London." She looked at him. "What do you want?"

Gray's brows shot up. "I? To see my paintings in the Royal Academy. To study in Rome and paint among the masters. To beat my brother Will in a horse race, and to win back the twenty quid I lost to my mate Tom Wayles-Faire." *To know your heart gives the same leap of joy mine does, every time you smile at me,* he added silently.

He was in grave danger of falling in love with her. She tidied his studio every day, but without putting anything where he couldn't find it. She did chores around the house even though he knew she was a well-born lady. She drew hedgehogs on scraps of paper and hummed on the stairs. Gray had never known one woman who could be so fascinating, charming, and yet not demanding in the slightest.

"The Academy!" She smiled. "I'm certain that will happen. You would set Rome on its ear, and I'm sure Will cheated when he beat you…"

Gray threw back his head and laughed. "No doubt!"

Samantha laughed, too, and then started to rise. Gray held out his hands. She took them, but staggered as she climbed awkwardly to her feet. Gray leapt out of his chair and caught her just before she toppled over. "I have you," he said, but his voice stuck in his throat as she looked up at him.

"You always seem to catch me," she said

ruefully. But she didn't make any effort to retreat from his grasp.

"It was my fault for asking you to kneel for so long." He inhaled slowly. "Do you remember what I said about trouble?"

Her eyes darkened, and she raised her face. "Mm-hmm."

"I'd no idea how much trouble I meant," he murmured. And then he kissed her.

He didn't want this woman to leave. She was the best parts of a muse, a friend, and a temptress, in one curvaceous package. And the way she kissed him back this time blew away all his notions of being a gentleman.

"Theater," he said, breathing hard. "Dancing. That can be arranged…"

"Truly?" Her eyes shone.

"If you won't mind my escort."

"No," she murmured. "That would make it even better."

CHAPTER TEN

Samantha was helping Jenny with the mending when the front door banged the next day. Only Gray did that, to Mrs. Willis's eternal disapproval, but even he didn't usually come pounding up the stairs shouting her name. "Samantha!"

For a moment her heart stopped. She met Jenny's wide-eyed gaze, paralyzed. What had happened? Gray sounded frenzied. She rushed into the corridor, heart in her throat, just as he reached the landing. "What is it?"

His face was alive with excitement. "Good news! No—Splendid news!" He thrust a piece of paper at her. "The Academy's accepted two of my paintings."

She gasped, in relief and delight. "Two! Oh, Gray, how wonderful!"

"It's a bleeding miracle!" He seized her in his arms and swung her around. "Two of the four! A mate of mine, Thomas Wyles-Fair, has been painting even longer than I have, and never had even one accepted."

"Is this the first time you've submitted?"

His face was fierce with elation. "Yes." He caught sight of Jenny, hovering in the doorway behind her. "Jenny, we're having beef tonight. Run to the market and fetch a joint." He dug out a coin and handed it over.

"Aye!" She sped past them, calling to her aunt.

"You'll come see them, won't you?" Gray asked. He still held one of her hands.

Samantha hesitated. The Royal Academy was at Somerset House, only a few minutes' walk away. Walking into a gathering of artists and their patrons would run an enormous risk. Not only did many of the members know her father, there was a chance the earl himself would attend. He often did, and she knew he was in London—looking for her. All her pleasure for Gray's achievement drained away at the thought of coming face to face with

155

Stratford. "Wouldn't you rather escort your mother?" she parried. "You said it would make her so proud. Is she a great patroness of the arts?"

"Yes," said Gray. He'd clearly sensed her discomfort. "But will you?"

Having a painting accepted to the summer exhibition was a great honor; having two accepted, on his first submission, would put Gray's name on everyone's lips. It was a magnificent moment for him and she feared she was spoiling it—and yet how much worse it would be if she came face to face with her father there…

"Samantha?" Gray prodded.

On the other hand, how likely was it the earl would attend at the same moment she did? The exhibition was usually crowded, and Stratford hated crowds. He would have no reason to suspect she would be there. And it would please Gray, which would please her more than she cared to think about. She wanted to go, and too many times she had denied herself because of what her father wanted. "Very well," she murmured with a nervous smile. "Yes."

His expression eased back into a wide smile, and she realized he had grown as tense as she had. He raised her hand and kissed her knuckles. "Thank you," he whispered, just as Mrs. Willis came panting up the stairs, exclaiming over his generosity about the beef and gushing about the news that two paintings, done in her own house, would be exhibited at the Royal Academy.

Gray must have sensed her apprehension about going, though, for only a few days later, as evening approached, he told her to put on her bonnet.

"Where are we going?" she asked as he offered her a shawl.

He grinned. "To see my paintings."

"They're already hanging?" The summer exhibition hadn't opened yet, even for private viewings.

"Perhaps not," he admitted, "but I want you to see them. The fellows who position the pictures said we could slip in for a few minutes tonight and see part of the selection."

157

Her heart felt tight. She ducked her head and tied the bonnet ribbons. He'd made a special arrangement for her, knowing she was hesitant to go when the rooms would be filled with people.

They walked to Somerset House, the former palace of queens and current home to the Royal Academy of Arts. Samantha had never been here, but various periodicals had featured engravings of the splendid arched entrance of the enormous mansion. Gray led her up a spectacular staircase, now cloaked in shadows, and then into a large room whose ceiling soared overhead, illuminated by the remnants of the sunset coming through the windows set into the very top of the walls. A few men stood in a cluster in the center of the room, pointing from time to time as they directed workmen hanging pictures high up on the walls.

Gray leaned down until his long hair brushed her cheek. "My mentor, Sir John Barney," he whispered, nodding toward a slim older man with receding gray hair, who raised a hand in greeting. The other gentlemen gave them barely a glance, too absorbed in their discussion. "Brilliant painter, and member of the selection committee. He gave us permission to come tonight."

"I'm very grateful to him," she whispered back, smiling.

"I wish it were more assembled, but come this way—he told me my work will be in this room." They went into the next room, smaller but still spacious and grand. Here more paintings had been hung, and she got a sense of how overwhelming the final exhibit must be. Pictures hung on nearly every inch of wall, up to the ceiling. The higher ones were angled down, in some cases looming over the viewer. Even in the fading light, it was stunning.

"Here we are." Gray stopped in front of a large canvas. It was a seascape, similar to the shipwreck painting in his studio, except it showed the ship leaving harbor, sails straining at the ropes, smaller boats darting around it, with passengers waving from the rail and sailors in the rigging. The light suggested the sun was rising behind the viewer, painting everything in a golden glow.

"It's magnificent," she breathed. The detail

was wonderful, the colors vibrant. "And on the line, too!" It hung right at eye level from the cornice that circled the room.

Gray grinned. "You noticed that, did you?"

"Of course!" She laughed. "You'll be elected a member before long."

They strolled around the room, taking in the other paintings. Samantha thought none were as fine as Gray's, but he praised each artist's style, technique, expression, and color composition. "There's something to learn from all of them," he told her, his voice echoing slightly in the empty room.

"You belong in their company," she answered. "I'm in awe."

They went through the doorway into another room, where some paintings were on the walls and some merely leaned against them. "There will be the other." Gray pointed above the doorway. "Sir John told me. It's a landscape, painted at Kirkwood, my family's seat in Lancastershire. Let me see, perhaps it's here…" He peered at various paintings leaning against the walls, finally locating it. "This is it."

She leaned over to examine the painting,

marveling again at his talent.

They left soon, as it had grown dark in the galleries. Samantha pressed his arm as they reached the street. "Thank you, Gray."

"Of course. I wanted you to see it."

She smiled wryly. "Thank you for bringing me tonight, before the crowds. It was wonderful."

He looked at her for a long moment. "For me as well—because you were with me." Then his face split into a grin. "And now we celebrate."

"What? Oh!" She gave a gasp of laughter as he surged forward, carrying her along with him into a nearby tavern, the Bull and Dog.

They burst onto a scene of exuberant merrymaking. "It's the Acceptance Ball," he shouted over the din. "Everyone with a work in the exhibition is welcome."

Samantha's dazed eyes wandered over the crowd. "All of these people are artists?"

"Or a friend of an artist," he said happily, "or just a stranger from the street. It's a celebration!" He pulled her into the room, calling greetings to various people, who lifted mugs of ale and shouted in reply. Several thumped him on the back, roaring with congratulations, and Gray returned them.

They found seats at a table, but not for long. Someone started playing a lively dance tune on a violin, and then a couple began dancing. Before long most of the room was on their feet, clapping or dancing, and Gray held out his hand in invitation. Samantha's heart skipped a beat. She'd never experienced such a party, where couples held each other shockingly close and romped through the packed room without regard for propriety or the form of any dance she recognized. "I don't know the steps," she told him.

He laughed. "There is no dance. Will you?"

She barely had time to nod before he caught her in his arms and swung her into the mad whirl. Around and around they went, bumping into people, laughing madly, barely able to hear the music. When they finally stopped, Samantha was gasping for breath, but thrilled to the very core. This was the most fun she'd ever had in her life, noisy and boisterous and uninhibited. The volume in the room could quaintly be called a roar.

Gray seemed to know everyone there. He introduced her to them all, but the names blurred into one. They squeezed onto a bench at the table the violinist stood on, stomping one boot on the wide planks as he played, and someone slid some tankards down to them. Gray was on his feet, singing along with the music in between gulps from his tankard. When Samantha wrinkled her nose at ale, a woman across from her pushed a small glass of clear liquid to her. Caught up in the moment, Samantha drank. Then she nearly coughed it all up as her nose and throat burned.

"What—gin!" Gray pounded on her back. "The first sip's the most potent."

Eyes streaming, she shouted back, "I'll remember that next time!" Grinning, the woman who'd given her the first glass passed her another, and mimed drinking it slowly. This time it went down easier, bringing a pleasant sense of lightness to the evening and helping her forget that she was an earl's daughter, drinking common gin with a motley pack of artists and musicians.

They danced again, even less adeptly than before, finally stumbling to an exhausted halt near the back wall. Samantha leaned against the rough plaster, her heart pounding and her face prickling with sweat, and thought she'd never been so happy.

Gray looked at her and laughed. Samantha laughed back. His arm was still around her waist and she could feel the thump of his heart against her shoulder. He was so vibrant, so full of joy tonight. It made her well-mannered life at Stratford Court seem like a fading bad memory, sterile and oppressed. She couldn't imagine going back to it now, and when Gray's hands touched her hips, shifting her against him so she fit under his arm more neatly, she turned into his embrace instead. His eyes sparkled beneath lowered lids, and then he was kissing her, his fingers molding to her jaw and his mouth ravishing hers.

Tonight she felt as wild and free as Constance in those wicked stories, and just as restless. Constance was a lady, just as she was, and if one lady could be wicked, so could another. Gray's arms around her made her shiver; his kiss made her melt. She went up on her toes and whispered, "Take me home."

His hand stroked over her back. "Already?"

She pushed her hands into his hair, the long strands damp and curling with perspiration. He smelled of paints and sandalwood and sweat, gloriously hot male. She tugged his head lower, closer to her own. "Take me to bed," she breathed in his ear.

For a moment Gray didn't move. She pressed her lips to the skin below his ear. It must be the gin, or the exercise, but she felt feverish with wanting. All her life she had been told this was *wrong wrong wrong,* but nothing had ever felt so urgently right.

"Are you certain?" he said against her ear. "Or is it the gin?"

The gin made her bold enough to say it, but the wanting… That had been building for days, through every hour she posed for the painting under his dark, intense gaze, through every night she slept in his bed and remembered the feel of his lips on hers. Her fingers clenched on his hair. "I'm certain."

He kissed her again, hard and joyful, then

seized her hand and plowed through the crowded tavern. He waved good-naturedly to anyone who called after them, but his steps didn't slow. During the brisk walk back to Stanhope Street he held her close to his side. Samantha didn't need to be urged along; her steps were as quick as his, and every few minutes they exchanged searing glances. At Number Eight, Gray dropped the latchkey twice before inserting it into the lock, swearing as Samantha giggled at his clumsiness. He banged the door shut more quietly than usual, then followed hard on her heels up the stairs, past Mrs. Willis's apartments to his rooms, now Samantha's.

Neither took the time to light the lamps. Gray turned the key in the lock with one hand and reached for her with the other. He kissed her again, bearing her backward through the sitting room and into the bedroom. There he set her down on her feet and held her at arm's length. "Samantha, perhaps we should stop—"

"Why?" She reached up and unbuttoned her spencer. His eyes tracked her fingers' progress down the front of the garment and his hands fell away from her elbows as she peeled it off.

"Uh." With a flinch he jerked his gaze back up to her face. "It's not proper for a lady to…" He made a vague motion that caused her to blush.

But her blood was still running, and she couldn't get rid of the thought of holding him, his beautiful artist's hands on her skin. Deep down Samantha knew that these weeks with him had wrecked her—she could never go back to her quiet life now, not when she would carry the memory of Gray in her heart forever. Unlike Philip, he was everything she'd ever dreamed of in a man, and even if he didn't feel the same way about her, she would never regret this.

"Nothing I've done lately has been proper," she said softly. "And I've never been happier. It's not gratitude or the gin. The truth is that I—I think I've fallen a little bit in love with you, and I want you."

His eyes were almost black, and his breath shuddered in his chest. "Love?"

Her face heated. "I—I don't expect that you feel the same—"

He seized her face in both hands and kissed her. "You have expressed my feelings perfectly, as it turns out." One hand wandered down her back and began loosening her dress's fastening. "The Lord above knows I've wanted you since the moment I saw you strolling down the Strand."

"Is that why you—?"

"No," he said, cutting off her question. "I would have come to your aid had you been wizened and hideous."

She tugged at the loose end of his neckcloth. "I was going to ask if that's why you offered me your own rooms."

"Oh," he said. "Well, yes."

She laughed and he dropped his head, whispering kisses alone the bared slope of her shoulder. "You're so lovely," he murmured, his breath heating her skin. Her dress slid down her shoulders and his hands followed, pushing the cheap cotton lower until she pulled her arms free of the sleeves and it puddled on the floor around her feet.

Blindly she struggled with his clothing. Unlike the loose shirts and smocks he'd worn at first, tonight he was fully dressed, and the construction of men's clothing was foreign to her. His coat came off, then the waistcoat with a little more effort, and she almost exclaimed aloud when he yanked the hem of his shirt free of his trousers and pressed both her hands to his stomach. He went still as her fingers tentatively explored his hot skin.

"You're so warm," she marveled. "So strong."

Gray swallowed. He still gripped fistfuls of shirt, and finally stripped it over his head. "Not where you're concerned, Perdita." He stepped closer and she went willingly, running her hands over his chest and shoulders. Her corset came loose and she barely noticed.

"I don't feel lost anymore," she told him.

He lifted her and carried her to the bed, laying her down as gently as he might a sleeping child. "You're never lost with me," he whispered, stretching out beside her on the coverlet.

She felt found. Saved. Loved. He tugged the ribbon of her chemise loose, finding the soft weight of her breast. Every touch of his hands

169

made her sigh and long to twine herself around him, especially when his palm slid up the side of her thigh.

"Samantha," he breathed, inching her chemise higher. "Do you know... Do you understand...?"

"Making love?" she panted. "Yes."

He gulped. His hand shaped to her hip, his thumb tracing circles on her belly. "Right. If you want me to stop..."

Her heart swelled. "I would tell you."

He nudged her legs apart, until Samantha simply hooked her left leg over his hip. It was bold and shocking and so wonderful, as Gray cupped his hand between her thighs and stroked the aching pulse there. His kiss stole her gasps of pleasure, his arm anchored her as she writhed. She felt something building inside her, frightening and addictive, and when he pressed one finger inside her, tears leaked from her eyes.

Gray rolled them both over until he sprawled atop her, his weight pushing her knees farther apart. "You're so soft," he rasped. He tore at the buttons of his trousers, shedding the clothing he still wore, and then she felt him against her.

He pushed himself up on one arm so he could adjust himself with the other hand; Samantha tensed as he pushed; he stroked her again and a shock ran through her as he pressed forward until his hips fit snugly between her legs.

Time paused. She shifted beneath him, no longer caught up in the drowning pleasure, but distracted by the feeling of him inside her. Gray flinched, then pulled back and pushed deep again. "Don't move," he said in a strained voice. "Just…let me love you…" He licked his thumb and parted the damp curls between her legs to settle on that pulse again.

This time each swirl of his thumb set off shocks through her limbs. She clung to him, dimly aware that Gray was moving, his spine flexing as he slid in and out of her, crooning words she was too frantic to understand. That feeling was building again inside, as if she were racing up an endless flight of stairs, her breath growing shorter until she reached the top—

And plunged over. She convulsed with a little cry, the blood roaring in her ears. Gray's head dropped onto her shoulder; his arms trembled; and his hips thrust hard against hers.

Samantha stared, wide-eyed, at the ceiling. Gray still shuddered in her arms and she felt his lips moving on her skin. They were wrapped around each other, naked and sweating, his flesh inside her body, and she'd never felt better in her life. An incredulous smile curved her lips as she turned her head to kiss him.

"I'm crushing you," he mumbled. He rolled to the side without relaxing his hold on her.

"No." She stroked the hair back from his face. "Do you remember what I said earlier? About being a little bit in love with you?"

His eye opened, gleaming at her like a cat's.

"I lied," Samantha whispered, touching the corner of his mouth. "I'm more than a little bit in love with you."

"Good," he murmured back. "Because I'm utterly mad about you, my darling."

CHAPTER ELEVEN

She awoke alone in bed. Sunlight seeped through the curtains, and when she stretched there was an unfamiliar but delicious ache in her body. A smile seemed permanently fixed on her face, and she hummed as she dressed and went down for breakfast.

The next few days passed in the same rosy-tinged glow. Gray invited her to the studio to pose for him, but each time he ended up making love to her on the chaise instead, Samantha muffling her cries in his shoulder. At moments she wondered at herself; just weeks ago she had been too frightened even to tell him her name and now she could hardly refuse him anything. She had transformed into an entirely different person in Stanhope Street, and she liked her new self very much.

Everything about her old life seemed gone, and she deliberately tried not to think of it. To think about it would be to face the reality that she was a runaway who could not stay in Stanhope Street forever. The thought of leaving brought her physical pain, not only for the unpleasant question of where she would go.

It was impossible not to think of the best option. Gray had said it himself: she could marry another chap. He had also said he was mad about her and made love to her. It wasn't hard to draw a line between those two points, connect it to the fact that she was head over heels in love with him, and wind up at the blissful idea that she could marry *him*.

That would be wonderful...for her. For him, she didn't know. By running away from home, she had stained her own reputation irreparably. By marrying a man other than the one her father chose, she had almost surely lost her dowry. For all his unconventional ways, Gray was still a duke's son. Even if he didn't care about those two enormous faults, his family might. In wistful moments she wondered about them, the indulgent duke who said he wanted a daughter and the duchess whose tears could keep four unruly sons in line. What would they say about her?

She found out when Gray slipped into her bedroom very late one night. She woke when he slid into bed beside her, murmuring a soft reassurance as he pulled her into his arms. She sighed happily and nestled against him. He'd been out all day and evening.

"Samantha," he breathed. "Are you awake?"

She smiled and lifted her face, eyes still closed. "Perhaps…"

Gray dropped a brief kiss on her lips. "I have something to tell you."

Her eyes flew open.

"Nothing alarming," he assured her. "Good news. I wrote to my mother and told her about you."

Now she was tense, hardly able to breathe.

"I knew you had nowhere to go, so I asked her to come to town and sponsor you. She wrote back that of course she would. They arrive tomorrow, and you will be a welcome guest in their house for as long as you want to be."

She wet her lips. "Even though… Do they know about this?" Each word had become more hesitant. When Gray wrote to his mother, Samantha had been a fugitive; now she was his lover, and the duchesses Samantha knew would never take a fallen woman into their homes.

"No, I didn't write to tell my mother about *this*." Gray grinned, although it quickly faded. "But I would like… That is, I hope…" He cleared his throat. "Once you are installed there and resume using your proper name and rank, I would like to court you."

Her mouth fell open.

"If you would rather I don't, you would still be welcome with my mother," he hastened to add. "But—"

"Yes," she whispered. "Please."

His smile was wonderful. "Of course you might meet other fellows more to your liking, but either way you'd have your choice. And if you did choose me, well… I'm not a terrible catch. You've only ever mentioned your father, but you must have other family, whom you must miss. A decent match might ameliorate his anger and allow you to be accepted back—"

She flung herself at him, cutting off the last. *"Yes.* You'd be a wonderful match, Gray, for me or for any woman."

Now sprawled on his back with her on top of him, he grinned. "I only care about you. Enough that I give you leave to call me George."

"George." Her lips curved. "I thought you hated the name."

"Say it again." He pretended to listen very closely as she repeated it several times. "I like it much better when you say it. Who knew everyone else says it wrong?"

The next day was Varnishing Day, when the artists were to apply the final coats of varnish in preparation for the exhibition. Gray packed up his materials and departed for the Academy, whistling. Samantha bid him farewell, feeling buoyant with joy.

She went up to the studio. Now that Gray had paintings at the Summer Exhibition, she was certain dealers would be coming by to see his work. Those buyers routinely came to

Stratford Court to show her father pieces in hopes he would purchase them. A neat and tidy studio would reflect well on Gray, but he left everything where it was when he used it, leading to wild disarray.

She had been at work for almost two hours when the knock sounded on the front door. With the windows open, it was easily heard even four floors away. She didn't pay attention to the sound of Jenny's voice answering the door, and was startled when the girl rapped on the studio door. "Miss…"

"Yes?" In the middle of organizing paint pots, Samantha looked up. Jenny stood in the doorway, fiddling anxiously with the strings of her apron, and behind her…

Samantha stopped breathing as her father brushed by the terrified maid and stepped into the room. It seemed an eternity since she had seen him; she at least felt a new person. But as his arctic gray eyes slid over her, she was abruptly aware that he had not changed one whit. For a moment her brain raced. Could she charge by him and run? She knew the way out the back of the house and might even make it to the market...

His gaze landed on her. His expression didn't change. Samantha raised her chin and didn't say a word. The time to run was past.

"I hardly dared believe it, when Milner said he had seen you at the Academy." Stratford's tone was cool and idle. He closed the door on Jenny and prowled across the room, hands clasped behind his back. "Surely not, I thought; my daughter must have been taken hostage, held somewhere against her will. Surely it could not be she on the arm of some stranger, promenading brazenly through Somerset House. Not after she disappeared so shockingly, throwing her mother into a fit of grief and worry."

Her fingernails were digging into her palms, but still Samantha said nothing. This was the earl's way, to cut and wound and turn her natural affections and sensibilities against her.

"But here she is," finished Stratford softly. His glance swept around the room. "Living in squalor."

In the ringing silence, Samantha could hear Mrs. Willis exclaiming in protest downstairs.

Stratford must have brought servants with him to enforce his will. "What are they doing to Mrs. Willis?" she asked.

The earl stared at her.

"The landlady," Samantha clarified. "She's been very kind to me and it would be dishonorable to abuse her."

Slowly he took a step closer, so close she had to tip her head back to keep meeting his eyes. Her heart thudded painfully against her ribs. He might not be shouting or waving his hands about, but her father was livid. "You would do well," he said in a low voice, "to think of your own circumstances at the moment."

You're of age, whispered Gray's voice in her mind. *I want to court you.* "I was thinking of my own circumstances, Father, when I fled Richmond."

At the bold confession the earl rocked back on his heels. Samantha thought—knew—he must have been quite certain of it, but he hadn't expected her to admit it. "Indeed."

Her heart was in her throat, but she didn't look away. "I will not marry Lord Philip."

Rage flared in his face. "You'll do as you're

told."

She shook her head. "Not that. I'm of age, and I—"

He raised his hand and she couldn't stop her flinch. Instead of striking her, he took her chin in his fingers. Now she couldn't look away. "When I sign a contract, I see that it is honored. You are my daughter, my property, and you will wed the man I choose. None of this childish nonsense—"

"He is cruel and vicious," she said, interrupting him for the first time in her life. "He would most likely kill me within a year, and how would that reflect on your wisdom in making the alliance?"

His fingers tightened. "If you are a meek and compliant wife, he will treat you properly. If you behave as you've done recently, any man would discipline you."

Not Gray. Gray would risk his life to save her and disrupt his life to help her. With a small jerk of her head, Samantha pulled free of the earl's grip and took a step backward. "I tell you now, on *my* word of honor, if you try to marry me to Philip, I would consider it akin to the bonds of slavery and do everything in my power to flee, no matter the scandal."

Stratford's face had never been more terrifying, stony and dark. "I will not tolerate this—"

"I'm not a maid any longer," she blurted out. "Lord Dorre won't want me for his daughter-in-law."

"Who?" said her father after a shocked moment of silence.

"Every man on the street," Samantha lied. "Every chance I got, I gave myself to anyone who would make me undesirable because *I will not marry Lord Philip.*" She was out of breath by the end, alarmed and exhilarated by the way she was standing up to her father. "Or anyone else not of my choosing," she boldly added for good measure.

All the expression dropped from Stratford's face. "Come," he said in a low voice. "Come with me now, or I will have you dragged from the house. Do not try my patience any longer, Samantha."

Still breathing like a racehorse, she hesitated, thinking of the servants who must be waiting outside the door. She would lose if it came to a battle. "Where?"

"To Portland Place. Your mother—whose feelings you seem to have utterly disregarded in your willful disobedience—is there, weeping daily over your absence."

Mama. Samantha felt a wave of remorse, even though she tried to steel herself against it. Stratford had always been willing to use affection as a weapon. "Very well. I will go to see Mama."

He stepped back and waved one hand toward the door. Three burly footmen were standing, expressionless, on the landing, and they closed ranks around her as soon as she stepped out of the room. "This way, my lady," said one, nodding toward the stairs.

She thought of saying something to Mrs. Willis, who was peering fearfully from the parlor door, but she didn't dare leave a message for Gray. The landlady would tell him what happened, and he would figure it out. Uncomfortably aware that she no longer had any choice in the matter, she went out to the carriage, and let the footman waiting there help her in. Four footmen plus a driver. Stratford *would* have had her dragged from the house.

But he himself did not come out. "Where is my father?" she asked the footman. The man's eyes were filled with sympathy, but he didn't reply. Her skin prickled with unease. She sat back against the squabs and stared out the window. Gray wasn't expected back for hours, but she suddenly wished he would come sooner.

The bell at St. Mary-le-Strand tolled the hour before Stratford finally emerged and climbed into the carriage. Samantha's nerves had been worn thin. "What kept you?" she asked.

He gave her a curiously expressionless glance before facing ahead without a word. The carriage started off at once, and Samantha gripped her hands together, knowing that things had taken a very bad turn.

Gray came home with a spring in his step. His pictures were freshly varnished, hung in very propitious spots. The harbor scene was near several works by RA members, ensuring it would be seen by everyone. The landscape had been hung just above a door, commanding the attention of everyone leaving. It was a triumph for a new artist to the exhibition. He couldn't wait to tell Samantha. The exhibit would last several weeks, and he longed to take her again, to view his paintings in daylight as they were meant to be seen.

Of course, he wanted to take her everywhere. His parents were to arrive in town today, meaning he could escort Samantha there this evening. His mother would sponsor her, his father would protect her, and he… He could call on her. Court her. He'd got the horse a bit before the cart, but only because she kissed him and smiled at him and that drove every rational thought from his mind, but that didn't change his fundamental goal: winning her.

He let himself into the house and ran up the first flight of stairs before realizing it was dead silent in the house. His steps slowed; that was odd. Mrs. Willis hadn't called her usual lament when he let the door bang, and it gave him a strange sense of foreboding.

He located his landlady in the kitchen. She

sat at the wooden table, sniffling into a handkerchief as Jenny and Cook hovered over her. At his entrance, she exclaimed out loud. "Oh, my lord! Thank heaven you're back!"

"What's happened?" he demanded. "Where is Samantha?" She was the only one missing, and the foreboding blossomed into fear.

"Her father came for her." Mrs. Willis's eyes were red. "He spoke to her, and she went straight out to the carriage. But he—he—" Another fit of weeping overcame her, and she collapsed into Cook's arms.

Gray turned toward Jenny. "Well?"

"Oh sir! Such a to-do!" She swelled with importance, delighted to be imparting the news. "He walked right in as if he owned the house, he did, and closed himself in the studio with Miss Samantha. Then she went out to the carriage, without so much as a fare-thee-well to Mrs. Willis or me, and then he started asking questions. So many questions! About who lived here, and how long Miss Samantha had been here, and every little thing you could think of. Then he went upstairs and took his own time up there, sir, in your rooms and studio—"

"What the devil?" Gray scowled.

The girl nodded vigorously. "Mrs. Willis protested that, sir, but he'd brought men with him—big chaps, all of them, and they wouldn't let us out of the sitting room."

"Imprisoned in my own home!" wailed the landlady as Cook patted her shoulder.

"And then he come back down and they all left, without a gentle word or apology." Jenny shook her head in disgust. "And him a proper lord!"

"Who was it?" The simple act of breathing made Gray's whole body vibrate. *"Who,* Jenny?"

"Lord Stratford, one of the servants called him."

"The Earl of Stratford?" Gray was astonished. He knew of the earl. A devoted patron of the arts, Stratford was known for his keen eye and generous sponsorship. Just today a painter working next to him had expressed a hope that his picture would catch Lord Stratford's attention and win a nod of approval.

But Samantha feared him. He frowned. "He went up to my rooms?"

Jenny nodded. Gray thanked her and took

the stairs two at a time. Nothing looked amiss in the studio when he flung open the door. A sudden thought made him lunge for the sketchbook, but everything was still within, all the sketches he'd made of Samantha, even the one of her asleep in his bed, her curls tumbling around her bare shoulders. He went back to the kitchen. "When did they leave?"

"Hours ago," Jenny said.

"Oh, my lord, will I be arrested?" cried Mrs. Willis. "I'd no idea, none, that she was a lady, or a runaway!"

Gray thought that was nonsense, but he assured her he didn't think she'd be in trouble. Back through the house he went, out the door, into the twilight. Sir John Barney might still be at the Academy, and he would know Lord Stratford. Gray wasn't sure what to make of the conflicting reports; was Stratford the urbane art patron, austere and demanding but still respected, or the cold and vindictive parent Samantha described, who would wed her to a man she feared?

By good fortune he met Sir John on the staircase of Somerset House. Before he could even ask, though, his mentor gave him a grim look and waved him back down the steps. Once they reached the pavement outside, Sir John stopped. "Bad news, my boy."

Gray's eyebrows went up.

"Your paintings have been removed from display."

"What?"

Sir John nodded. "By order of the president of the Academy, just minutes ago. I was coming to find you."

"Why?" Gray couldn't have been more shocked if his mentor had punched him in the gut. "I was here an hour ago and they were on the walls—"

"And now they are not." Barney lowered his voice. "Have you done something untoward? It must have been a serious reason to make the president order such a change so soon before the exhibit. They've got men rearranging pictures at this very moment, it's a terrible inconvenience."

Gray was staggered. His paintings, freshly varnished and hung in such prime positions, taken down. He'd never met the president of the Academy, Benjamin West; what could have led to this?

"Stratford," he said numbly.

Barney raised his brows. "The Earl of Stratford? What about him?"

"Could he have asked West to take them down? If he asked, would West do it?"

"I suppose he might," said Sir John in surprise. "Stratford's a great patron of the Academy and many members; West would likely listen to his request. But why would he do that? I didn't know you were acquainted with His Lordship."

"I'm not."

"Then why the devil would Stratford want your paintings taken down?"

Gray barely heard the question. He made no answer, but he knew. It could only have been Stratford, who had taken Samantha, questioned Mrs. Willis to the point of tears, and gone into his studio. The cathedral painting was in full view on his easel and while Gray thought her image was small enough not to be identifiable, her father might well recognize her. It could only have been the furious and vengeful man

Samantha described.

And there was only one place he could turn for help. Not for his paintings, but for Samantha.

The Rowland mansion was ablaze with light when he reached Berkley Square. The door stood open as footmen carried trunks inside, so he walked right in, nodding in reply to the butler's startled greeting.

His mother was in the drawing room, still in her traveling dress. "George!" she exclaimed, raising her cheek for his kiss. "How punctual you are."

"I need help, Mother."

She gave him a patient glance. "Yes, I know. It's why we've returned to town in spite of your father spying a large number of geese just a week ago. He's been pining for the fine shooting he's missing."

"I've met a lady."

Her teasing smile vanished at his tone; her expression snapped to alertness. He could almost see her nose twitch like a hound's when

191

tracking a fox. The duchess's fondest wish was to see all four of her sons happily married. "A lady."

"The lady I asked you to come to town to sponsor. She needs my help, and that means I need your help."

With a swish of her skirt, she went to the settee and sat down. "Explain."

He had just made it through the story when the duke walked in. "George! Hodgkin told me you were here. How the devil are you, my boy?"

"He hasn't come to visit," said his wife.

Rowland narrowed his eyes. "Then why?"

Gray ran his hands over his hair. "I must see the Earl of Stratford."

"Stratford!" The duke rolled his eyes. "I'd avoid him, if I were you. What do you want with that tartar?"

Gray gave his mother an agonized look. "Go on, dear," she said, patting his knee.

"I had two paintings accepted to the Summer Exhibition," he began.

"Two—but that's brilliant!" The duke beamed. "Well done! Eliza, did you know about this?"

The duchess shook her head, eyes still fixed on Gray, who took a deep breath before continuing. "They won't be on exhibit. They were taken down just today; Sir John Barney told me himself, he saw the men rearranging pictures." The duke looked thunderstruck. Gray forged on. "I believe the Earl of Stratford asked President West to order it. He's very influential at the Academy."

"Why would Stratford want to remove your pictures from display?" Rowland growled. "He's a cold one, but anyone can see you've got talent to spare, I'm surprised they only accepted two…"

Involuntarily Gray smiled. How like his father. Normally his painting left his father somewhat puzzled, appreciative but uncomprehending; but the moment someone else slighted his work, Rowland became the most ardent and impassioned defender of it. Gray hoped the same instinct would motivate his father now. "It may be because of his daughter."

The duke squinted. "What?"

"I'm in love with Lord Stratford's daughter,"

Gray said softly. "And I want to marry her."

CHAPTER TWELVE

It was not difficult to find the Earl of Stratford's London house. It was one of the finer homes in Portland Place, seven windows wide and built of clean white stone. The broad boulevard didn't offer much concealment, but Gray found a tree where he could linger and still have a view of the house.

His father had warned him not to do anything until the morrow, but Gray couldn't possibly spend the night in Stanhope Street, listening to Mrs. Willis fret about being arrested. He promised himself he would only watch, and leave as soon as he caught a glimpse of Samantha.

He watched and waited. The lamps were lit and the windows glowed, but there was no sign of inhabitants. *Walk across the room,* he silently wished. *Let me see that you're well.*

It had grown quite dark by the time God heard him. Cold and starving, Gray was about to leave. He only meant to dart over a few streets and get something to eat, since Portland Place was free of any convenient pubs, but that was the moment Samantha stepped up to the tall windows of the first floor and gazed out in his general direction.

His breath caught at the sight of her. Dressed as befitted an earl's daughter, she was more beautiful than ever—but not like herself. It took him a moment to realize that she might have been a statue. Her expression was serene, but she seemed to stare at nothing, and there was something valiantly hopeless about the set of her shoulders. He thought of Jenny's report of several large servants herding her out the door, and knew Samantha was a prisoner in that mansion.

Fury burned in his chest. Without taking his eyes from her, he searched his pockets for a stray scrap of paper and pencil. He always had some, to take down any scene or idea when it might strike him. He flattened a piece on his forearm and sketched urgently, stealing frequent glances up at the window where she stood. *Stay,* he begged her, *just a few minutes longer…*

He scooped up an egg-sized stone from underneath the tree behind him and slipped across the street. He had no string—it would have to be folded—he twisted the loose edges of the paper around the stone as tightly as he could, took careful aim, and heaved the rock.

It shattered a pane of the window next to her. He fell back into the shadows, eyes glued to the Stratford house. Samantha had jumped away, but now he saw her bending down, one hand clutched to her breast, the other reaching toward the floor. He barely breathed, even though he knew he was mad to linger. The last thing he wanted to do was find himself explaining to a constable. She turned her head, as if speaking to someone behind her, and then she faced the window. This time, hope shone in her expression, and she pressed her fingers to her lips before someone pulled her away.

Gray knew she couldn't see him, but she'd found his message. A few moments later the door of the house burst open and a pair of footmen strode out, armed with clubs. He put his shoulders back and strode off with the air of insouciant arrogance that always served his father so well, and headed home to plan what he would say tomorrow.

Samantha strained her eyes into the dark night. He was out there, very near. She had almost leaped out of her skin when the window broke right beside her, but thankfully recovered her wits in time to spy the paper wrapped around the rock that had shattered the glass. There was something written on it in charcoal, the kind of charcoal Gray always had in his pockets. She managed to pluck it from the shards of glass before her mother rushed over and pulled her away.

"Come away from the window!" the countess cried. "You might have been cut to death!"

"No, I'm fine," she assured her mother, not adding that she had never been in any danger. Gray had thrown carefully. She stuffed the scrap of paper into her pocket under pretext of hunting for her handkerchief.

"What the devil?" Stratford strode into the room, eyes blazing.

"Someone threw a rock through the window," said his wife. "Samantha could have been badly hurt."

The earl gave her a hard glance. "Are you?"

She shook her head. "I stepped away just as it broke. It—it gave me such a start, though. Who would do such a thing?" Her voice wobbled at the end, but not from fear of the broken glass. The expression in her father's eyes sent a chill to her heart.

"Who, indeed," muttered the earl, transferring his attention to the shattered window. "Send two fellows out and fetch anyone lurking about," he barked at the hovering butler. "Now, before the villain escapes!" The butler nodded and fled.

Stratford turned to her. "I don't suppose you saw anything," he said with quiet menace. "Someone outside in the street, perhaps?"

"I saw nothing," she said truthfully. She'd been sunk in misery and hadn't even thought to look for Gray. The crumpled paper in her pocket felt as big as a boulder but it also seemed to glow with warmth. He had found her and followed her. Even if the paper only held a sad farewell, it was something of him.

"Nothing," Stratford repeated. His mouth shifted into something resembling a smile, albeit a cold and angry one. He didn't believe her. "Retire to your room, my dear, to recover from the shock you've just received. I shall find the ruffian who did such a thing and see him thrown into jail."

She nodded. "Yes, Father." She wasn't terribly afraid for Gray—even if her father could prove he'd thrown the rock, Samantha trusted the Duke of Rowland to keep his son out of prison. Right now it was far more important her father not discover the paper.

Her mother escorted her to her room, directing her maid to pull the drapes. "Bring Lady Samantha a cup of tea," the countess told the maid, sending the girl flying from the room. "Are you sure you're well?"

Samantha nodded.

Her mother's eyes were worried. "You don't think…" She lowered her voice to a bare whisper. "Could it have been someone you encountered on your misadventure?"

On the drive to Portland Place, Samantha had realized a few hard facts. First, that she could never tell anyone the full truth of what had happened to her. Twice now she had honestly confessed to her father, and it had done her no good; from now on she meant to tell as wild and incredible a story as she could imagine, and hope it would torment him.

Second, she must not let him use her heart against her. She couldn't breathe a word of Gray's assistance, or her father would ruin him. Samantha felt like crying at the thought of giving him up entirely, though, and vowed to find a way to see him. She meant what she'd said to her father: if he tried to make her marry Lord Philip, she would run away again and again, to Gray if possible, but anywhere else if not. Now that she'd had a real taste of love and pleasure, Samantha thought she'd rather throw herself into the ocean than wed someone like Philip.

And third, she needed to keep the truth from her mother. The countess had sent for

Stratford when Samantha disappeared from
Richmond, and she was waiting in Portland
Place after the tense carriage ride from
Stanhope Street, tearfully relieved to have her
daughter home safe. If Samantha explained
what she had been "rescued" from, her mother
would feel terrible.

"Oh!" She widened her eyes, as if such a
thought had never occurred to her. "No! I can't
imagine it was. I thought surely it was more
likely someone who disagrees with Father about
emancipation." Thanks to her weeks of
freedom, she knew her father was a strident
voice of opposition to the emancipation bill
being advanced by reformers.

Lady Stratford blanched. "You may be
right." She paused, as if thinking. "I think you
quite likely are *exactly* right. Who else would
resort to such criminal tactics? Your father will
realize it as well, once he considers the
possibility."

Samantha nodded. "No one of any gentility.
It must be rabble-rousers."

Her mother let out her breath. "I'm so glad
to have thought of that. For a moment I

feared— But it was merely panic! My heart nearly stopped when I thought you might have been hurt." She embraced Samantha and kissed her cheek. "Sleep well, my dear."

"Thank you, Mama."

She closed the door behind her mother and leaned against it. Hardly breathing, she groped in her pocket. It was a coarse bit of paper, but it unfolded to reveal a familiar character: the rakish skunk had become a warrior, his fur bristled and his teeth bared. He was down on his knees, a sword clutched in his paws in the manner of a knight pledging himself. To anyone else it would look like a bit of rubbish, but Samantha gave a gulping sob of happiness at the sight. *"George,"* she whispered.

It was not farewell. He meant to fight for her.

CHAPTER THIRTEEN

Gray bounded out of the Rowland carriage the following morning.

"Not so quickly," muttered his father, climbing down the step behind him.

"I have to see her again." He'd barely slept all night, wondering if Samantha had interpreted his message correctly.

The duke grunted. "Be that as it may, I know Stratford well enough to know this: do not seem too eager. The more he knows you want something, the harder he'll make you work to get it."

Gray's jaw tightened, but he had asked for his father's help, and only an idiot would spurn the duke's advice. He wrestled his impatience into order and fell into step beside his father as the footman rapped the knocker.

"His Grace the Duke of Rowland," announced the footman when the butler opened the door. "And his son, Lord George Churchill-Gray."

"Your Grace," said the startled butler. "Your pardon—"

"Yes, yes," said Rowland, striding past the man as if it were his own house. "I know Stratford's here. We'll wait." The butler scrambled to direct them to a small morning room, and recovered his composure enough to bow his way out with a look of frosty disdain.

Gray prowled the room. It was spartan and immaculate, overlooking the street. "Sit," said his father. "George, sit down."

"If he's whipped her I won't be able to restrain myself." Reluctantly he took a seat.

"You can and you will." Rowland leaned back, stretching his legs out on front of him and clasping his hands over his belly. "You have come to make an honorable offer of marriage for the lady. I have come to show my approval of the union, even though I've yet to set eyes upon the bride." He bent a wry look on his son. "This is a ramshackle way to go about marriage."

Gray ran his hands over his head. "I know. I didn't intend to do it this way, but now there's no choice."

Rowland grunted. "Are you certain you know what you're getting into, setting your heart on Stratford's daughter?"

He did. He dug the heels of his hands into his eyes, and Samantha's sparkling eyes shone back at him, her blond curls sliding free of their knot as he swung her around the tiny confines of the Bull and Dog. Her soft voice whispered in his ear, pleading and encouraging and marveling all at once as he touched her. He felt her hands on his skin, recalled the taste of her mouth, and felt the flush of elation when he brought her to climax. "Yes," he said softly.

The duke was quiet for a moment. "It's rare enough you ask for my assistance, I can hardly refuse. God help a man in love."

"Father." Gray raised his head. "She's not at all like the earl." He glanced at the door and lowered his voice. "Once she's my wife, I won't let Stratford near her."

Rowland cocked one sandy eyebrow. "You

don't just marry the woman, you marry the family. This is not a romantic escapade, where the two of you throw off all connections and decamp to America. Mark my words: Stratford's not the sort to surrender what's his lightly."

Gray didn't expect a surrender. He'd fight a war for her, though, and if Samantha never wanted to see her father again, Gray would ensure she didn't.

They sat and waited. Eventually, just at the edge of having been left waiting for an insulting length of time, the butler returned. "His Lordship expresses his gratitude for your call today, but unfortunately he is unable to receive you at the moment—"

"We'll wait," said Rowland, still relaxed and unruffled in his seat.

The butler peered down his long, thin nose. "That will not be necessary, His Lordship bade me tell you. He regrets that he will be busy for some time."

Gray rose. "I daresay Lord Stratford would prefer to have this conversation in discreet privacy. We have come to do just that. However, if he prefers a scene, I'm willing."

The butler looked from one to the other and closed the door without a word.

Half an hour later they were shown into the study. The earl stood behind his desk, expressionless and collected. "Rowland." A very chilly smile touched his lips for a moment, and he bowed. "To what do I owe this unexpected pleasure?"

The duke returned the bow. "Stratford. My son, George." Gray bowed. "'Tis his business we've come on today, very happy business."

The earl's pale gray gaze moved to him.

Gray had decided to assume the earl had learned everything about Samantha's time in Stanhope Street, one way or another. Accordingly he met those arctic eyes squarely. "I would like permission to court your daughter Samantha, my lord."

For a moment the earl didn't react. Then he reached for the bell. "Send Lady Samantha down," he told the servant who appeared almost instantly.

His heart skipped a beat at her name. "Excellent thought," said the duke warmly. "Let the lady decide. It's her hand at stake, what?"

Stratford looked as if he'd eaten a lemon. "She will not decide. I have a question to pose to her."

Rowland just raised his brows. Gray kept his expression neutral. Several minutes later, the door opened and Samantha stepped in.

She was more beautiful than he remembered, in a pale green dress with a locket around her neck and her blond curls twisted up. Her eyes met his and Gray felt his lungs constrict. Even though she didn't smile, he could tell she was pleased to see him.

"Samantha," said the earl coldly. "Do you know this man?"

"Yes." A blush of color came into her cheeks.

"Indeed." The earl stepped from behind his desk. "Is he the man who aided and abetted your illicit flight from your family?"

"He is the man who saved me from villains and gave up his own apartment for my comfort and safety," she replied.

"Is he the man who took you to a common tavern and plied you with gin?"

"Yes," she answered. "And it was

209

wonderful."

Stratford stopped dead. "Is he the man who violated you?"

Gray scowled. The duke made a quiet, shocked noise. Samantha raised her chin. "No," she said, her voice clear and calm. "He is the man I love."

The earl's face hardened. "Nevertheless, he has not behaved as a gentleman. And you are betrothed to Lord Philip Osbourne, son of the Marquess of Dorre."

"I refuse to marry Lord Philip," said Samantha, now flushed. Her hands were in fists, though she had pressed them into the folds of her skirt.

"I'm here to make my own proposal of marriage," Gray said quickly. "One that is, I hope, more to Lady Samantha's liking."

Joy glimmered in her eyes. "Very much so."

"Well done!" Rowland pounded Gray on the shoulder. "Shall we settle the terms?" he said to Stratford.

Gray glanced at the earl. Now he saw why Samantha had run, why she preferred to throw herself on the mercy of strangers rather than defy her father. Stratford was white-faced with rage, and Gray privately vowed never again to leave that man alone with Samantha. He looked like he could murder her.

"No."

The one word, clipped and icy, made them all start. "Tomorrow's just as good," said Rowland, recovering. "I'll send my solicitor—"

"No," repeated Stratford. "My answer to your offer of marriage, sir, is *no.*" Now he looked like he would murder Gray as well. Samantha darted an uncertain look at him, and Gray drew breath to argue.

"George," said the duke mildly, "escort Lady Samantha to another room. I fear my next comments shan't be fit for a woman's ears."

"How dare you," began the earl in a tight, furious voice.

Rowland turned toward Stratford. He was a big man, barrel-chested and broad-shouldered, while the earl was lean and wiry. Gray knew he was the most amiable man in the world, but when he wished to be, the duke could be a terrifying and imposing figure. "Let them go."

Stratford jerked in shock. Without looking

away from the earl, Rowland waved at Gray, who seized Samantha's hand and led her from the room.

"Oh my goodness," she whispered. "Oh my goodness!"

"Where can we wait?" he asked, and she pointed down the hall. Almost running, he pulled her into the small parlor, and barely shoved the door closed before she flung herself into his arms.

"You came!" She was laughing and crying at the same time. "You came for me!"

"Didn't you know I would?" He kissed her before she could reply. "The skunk—"

"I didn't know you would be here today!"

"As if I could wait." He untangled her arms from around his neck. "Since I've done nothing else properly, let me do this well." Retaining his grip on her hands, he went down on one knee. "My darling Samantha, will you marry me?"

Her smile trembled. "If my father—"

"He's going to consent," Gray promised her. "Why do you think I brought my father? Rather like calling in the heavy cavalry, that. I wasn't taking any chances."

She laughed, swiping tears from her cheeks. "Yes. Yes! I would run away with you if you asked."

He hauled her down for another kiss, and there was no more talking for a while.

When a servant opened the door to admit the duke, they were sitting on the sofa, hand in hand. Rowland came directly to Samantha. "I trust my son has pulled his wits together and proposed to you decently."

"He has."

Rowland's face softened. "Welcome to the family, my dear."

"He—he consented?" she gasped.

Rowland nodded. "With some conditions. Your dowry, I'm afraid, is not what a lady of your position deserves, but no matter. George, I will double your income. A married man must live properly."

Gray nodded, overcome with gratitude. That would give him four thousand a year.

"One of your paintings will be returned to the exhibition," Rowland went on. "I pressed for both, but then he began speaking of waiting a year for the wedding, and I suspected that would not be acceptable."

"Not at all," said Gray. The paintings could go to the devil.

"Thank you, sir." Samantha's voice was choked with emotion.

With a rather sly smile, the duke raised her hand to his lips. "The final condition is that I shall give away the bride. Stratford feels a strong desire to remove to his country estate at once."

Gray looked at Samantha. Her eyes were wide and dazed. "Then the wedding...?"

"Will take place as soon as George procures a license." He winked at his son. "Get yourself to Doctor's Commons, lad. I am going to purchase a wedding gift for my new daughter."

EPILOGUE

Eight days later
St. George's Church, Hanover Square

Samantha stepped down from the carriage and craned her neck, trying to see the clock near the base of the spire. "Are we late?"

Her brother raised a brow. "Do you think he wouldn't wait?"

"No." She gave him a stern glance. "I just don't want to be late. Is my dress crushed?" She turned so he could inspect her skirt.

"Not a bit. You look beautiful," Benedict told her. "But not because of the dress."

Samantha could only beam at him in helpless happiness. Gray had gone to see her brother as soon as he'd got the license, correctly guessing that Stratford would prevent her mother from attending. Lady Stratford had defied her husband enough to order Samantha's belongings packed and sent to her, but Stratford had made her accompany him back to Richmond. Elizabeth was too far away, and if not for Benedict, Samantha would have arrived at her wedding alone.

Some day, somehow, Samantha hoped to rescue her mother. This moment would be utterly perfect if only Mama were here to share her happiness. She strongly suspected, though, that her mother had gone quietly to Stratford Court to keep the earl from disrupting the wedding. As always, Lady Stratford put her children above herself.

"Are you pleased, Ben?" she asked, taking his proffered arm and starting up the steps at his side. "Do you approve?"

"I approve of him. I can't say it was the best idea to run away, but I am very pleased it's worked out so happily for you." He smiled ruefully. "May we all be so fortunate."

She squeezed his arm in silent agreement. They had reached the vestibule, where Rowland waited.

"I thought I was to escort the bride," he said jovially.

"I'll take my sister down the aisle," Benedict replied.

"Very good. I'll inform the impatient bridegroom that you have arrived." He glanced at the stunning pearl necklace Samantha wore, which he had bestowed on her the previous day. "They become you, my dear."

"Thank you, sir."

He opened his arms. "From today on, you may call me Papa—or any other nickname that takes your fancy."

Samantha caught her brother's shocked expression, but she stepped into the duke's light embrace and kissed his cheek. "Thank you, Papa." She'd never called anyone that.

He opened the sanctuary doors, and Samantha saw Gray—her George—waiting at the end. His three brothers stood with him, and the duchess sat near the front. It was real. Her throat felt tight and her heart was full to bursting. In an hour she would no longer be a Lennox, Lord Stratford's daughter, but Lady Samantha Churchill-Gray, wife of a painter with long hair and a ready laugh and the kindest heart she could imagine a man possessing. And he loved her, enough to take her with nothing. Stratford had revoked her dowry and was probably writing her out of his will at this moment.

Gray looked back and saw her. His head came up, and even from a distance she could see the wide grin on his face.

"Shall we go?" murmured Benedict. "Before he charges back here to fetch you himself?"

"Yes," she said, smiling broadly, and walked forward to meet her love.

THE SCANDALS SERIES

Don't miss a single scandalous moment…

SIX DEGREES OF SCANDAL
The last—and greatest—scandal of
all…unmasking Lady Constance.

LOVE IN THE TIME OF SCANDAL
Benedict Lennox needs a wife—but the most
likely bride is everything he never knew he
wanted in a woman.

IT TAKES A SCANDAL
Sebastian Vane is an outcast, unfit to marry an
heiress. But true love is no match for even the
darkest scandal.

LOVE AND OTHER SCANDALS
Tristan Burke isn't a marrying man—until a
droll, sharp-witted wallflower starts haunting his
dreams.

ALL'S FAIR IN LOVE AND SCANDAL
Douglas Bennet, notorious rake, makes a
scandalous wager—and loses his heart.

Caroline Linden was born a reader, not a writer. She earned a math degree from Harvard University and wrote computer software before turning to fiction. Since then, her books have won the NEC-RWA Reader's Choice Award, Daphne du Maurier Award, the NJRW Golden Leaf Award, and RWA's RITA Award. Visit her at *www.carolinelinden.com*.

Printed in Great Britain
by Amazon